THE
DUPLICATIONS

BOOKS BY KENNETH KOCH

Poems

Ko, or A Season on Earth

Permanently

Thank You and Other Poems

Bertha and Other Plays

When the Sun Tries to Go On

The Pleasures of Peace

Wishes, Lies, and Dreams:
Teaching Children to Write Poetry

A Change of Hearts:
Plays, Films, and Other Dramatic Works

Rose, Where Did You Get That Red?
Teaching Great Poetry to Children

The Art of Love

I Never Told Anybody:
Teaching Poetry Writing in a Nursing Home

The Duplications

THE
DUPLICATIONS

Kenneth Koch

RANDOM HOUSE   NEW YORK

To Katherine Koch

Copyright © 1975, 1976, 1977 by Kenneth Koch

All rights reserved under International and Pan-American
Copyright Conventions. Published in the United States by
Random House, Inc., New York, and simultaneously in
Canada by Random House of Canada Limited, Toronto.

Library of Congress Cataloging in Publication Data

Koch, Kenneth, 1925-
    The duplications.

    I. Title.
PS3521.O27D8   811'.5'4   76-53688
ISBN 0-394-40614-1
ISBN 0-394-73368-1 (pbk.)

Portions of this book were first published
in slightly different form in *Poetry, Georgia Review,*
Tri-Quarterly, Sun and *New York Arts Review.*

Manufactured in the United States of America

9 8 7 6 5 4 3 2

FIRST EDITION

THE
DUPLICATIONS

I

One night in Venice, near the Grand Canal,
A lovely girl was sitting by her stoop,
Sixteen years old, Elizabeth Gedall,
When, suddenly, a giant ice-cream scoop
Descended from the clouded blue corral
Of heaven and scooped her skyward with a loop-
The-loopy motion, which the gods of Venice
Saw, and, enraged, they left off cosmic tennis

And plotted their revenge. They thought some outer
Space denizen or monster had decided
To take this child, perhaps who cared about her
And wished to spare her heart a world divided,
Or else who wanted to hug, kiss, and clout her,
And, lust upwelling, the right time had bided,
Or something such—so thought, at least, the gods of
Her native city, famed for bees ar d matzoh.

Venice, Peru, of course, is where it happened,
A city modeled on the Italian one
Which was all paid for by Commander Papend,
A wealthy Yugoslav who liked his fun.
The Com had sexual urges large as Lapland
And was as set for action as a gun
In madman's hands who hates the world around him—
But Com was filled with love, his heart all pounding!

And so he'd made this North Italian jewel,
Canals and palaces on every side,
An urban re-creation, not renewal,
A daring lust's restatement of life's pride;
Huge bumboats carrying marble, masks, and fuel
Clogged South American streams, till Nature cried
"Some madman's building Venice in Peru!
Abomination beneath the sky's blue!"

In protest of his act, waves shook the earth:
Shock and resentment over this new Venice!
And Central South America gave birth
To hideous monstrous bees, so huge disfenes-
Tration would result when their great girth
Against some building window hurled its menace!
So, windowless new Venice had to be.
But there was one thing that could stop a bee

Of overwhelming size: a matzoh placard
Placed on the shoreside gilding of the house.
It must of course be large, huge as the Packard
Driven for Canada Dry by Mickey Mouse
Attempting to establish the world's record;
Minnie is at his side, and Gabby Grouse,
A brand new character who's been invented
Since Disney's death—they think he'd have consented.

Walt Disney dead! And Salvador Dali lives!
Paul Eluard gone, and Aragon still alive!
How strange the breathing tickets that fate gives—
Bees dance to show, when entering the hive,
Which way best flowers are, but are like sieves
To death's mysterious force. Oh you who drive
The car, stop speeding; breathe a little longer.
Create, and make us gladder now and stronger!

As Papend did by carrying out his plan
"Venice in South America," an almost
Perfectly accurate copy. Yet one can
Discern things here and there I think would gall most
Other Venetians: bees and the whitish tan
Enormous matzoh placards which some tall ghost
Might use for palace walls. O strange piazzas
Of South America, deranged by matzohs!

How was it known, you ask me, that the busy
Bees would stop marauding if confronted
With matzoh placards? Well, it makes bees dizzy
To look at matzoh. If more details are wanted,
See *Matzoh-Loving Bees* by E. McTizzy
Where all's explained: the stinger's slightly stunted
Or blunted, I forget, by the bakery pleating
Of the matzoh, made in this case not for eating

But civil defense. So with this problem over
Com could procede to build his city and bring
Into it thousands of young girls fresh as clover
And beautiful as an ancient Mexican ring
With jewels red as the hat of Smoky Stover,
And to these girls he offered everything
Our sad world can provide: drink, clothes, and money,
And, when he could, his love. Like some wild bunny

He made love over fifty times a day,
Never becoming sated, bored, or sleepy.
"It's just life's great experience," he'd say,
"That's all! Preferring other things seems creepy
When I can sweep into the disarray
Of limbs and golden hair, then plunge in deep. We
Live but once: let us not live in vain.
Sailors, come home! Here is life's bounding main!"

And, saying so, he'd lunge into some beauty
And, panting, pass a half an hour or so
Coming and crying "Ah, this is my duty!
Someone must make the human radar glow
Continually, or else the Cosmic Cutie
Will kill us! This I absolutely know!"
And so he'd theorize and love unceasingly
With pleasure growing in his soul increasingly.

Why did he want all this in Venice? Actually
I do not know. I'm not sure he did either.
I'd guess the city just aroused him sexually
As Mommy's breast arouses the pre-teether.
One's lust is bound by fancy, not contractually:
To rouse it even while one takes a breather
One needs an optimum spot, and so for Papend
The place was Venice—that's just how it happened.

He'd thought of Samos first, because he'd seen there
A beautiful city—he could not remember
Its name, but everything had been so green there
And the sea'd seemed a huge light emerald ember;
Also there was that temple to the Queen there
Of all Greek gods, even Hera; in September
He'd cabled to his manager in Split
To start creating Samos, that was it.

And then by chance, purely by chance one evening
He'd found himself in Venice, where the sheer
Beauty of everything set him to grieving
For having chosen Samos. It was queer
To change his mind so suddenly! but leaving
The cafe where he sat he phoned Vladmir
Komslavul with these words: "Abandon Samos!
Put Venice in its place. *Allons-y! Vamos!*"

.

And Venice had been born in old Peru,
A most unusual South American city
Where all Commander Papend did was screw
And give sweet things to girls, all of them pretty
As everything in nature is when new
And not decided on by a committee
But fresh and gravely formed by nature's process
Which shuns the minuscule and the colossus

In making human creatures—So, the gods
Decided to take vengeance on that scooper
Who'd taken the young beauty. "I'll give odds
It was some interplanetary snooper!"
Opined one other girl. "Our lightning rods
Do not keep off, as stun-ray keeps a grouper,
Strange alien eyes from gazing at our bodies
While we disrobe in Venice hall and cottage!"

It was discovered to have been, in fact,
No interplanetary plot but rather
What André Gide called "a gratuitous act"
Of cumulus clouds, which, when they are together
For a long time, sometimes overreact
And form some kind of scoop, which is a bother
If it behaves as this one did. The girl, though,
Was found unharmed though puzzled by her furlough

Among the clouds. Meanwhile in Greece, near lines
Which run from Theseus' temple to Poseidon's
Let's turn our gaze, like Heaven's, which divines
A motor vehicle with an inside ins-
Ide its outside larger than the spines
Of dinosaurs, which men with subtle guidance
From bits of bone and dust have put together
Inside museums to resist the weather

So we can walk around them saying, "Jesus!
What if them fuckers walked around today?"
And now and then a guard comes up and teases
Some little chap with "Did you see that, hey?
It moved! The thing's alive!" which so increases
The pleasure of the people there that they
Laugh to themselves at both the boy and guard—
So huge this automobile was. "Take a card,"

Said Minnie, as they drove, to Gabby Grouse;
"Mickey, how many do you have by now?"
"Dear, I can't play while driving. Here's the house!"
Gabbed Mick. "Look, dear," mouthed Minnie,
    "Clarabelle Cow
Is cropping grass as evenly as a louse
Creeps through the hair of evening. And a bough
Heavy with honeysuckle hangs above
Our nest of nozzling and our lair of love!"

"Truer were never spoken mousie words!"
Sang Mickey as he drove the gleaming Packard
Into the barn. Above him busy birds
Conduct their songfest, and not one is laggard.
"Clarabelle's milk has been too full of curds!"
Cries Pluto, running to them. Thought a faggot
By some, this dog was said to favor fellas
Of every species when he lived in Hellas.

But Mickey didn't give a damn! He smacked
Pluto between the ears and gave a whistle!
Clarabelle Cow came munching up. Mick whacked
Her on the ass and said, "I picked this thistle
In far-off Zululand, my love. Half-cracked,
I've brought it from that bush like an epistle,
Clarabelle Cow, for you! Now, food and rest!
Tomorrow we must be at our rodent best!

Come on! We've got to get this car unpacked
No time for fooling now; we have one night
And one night only, one, to be exact,
One twelve-hour span to seek our souls' delight
And then before Greece's hellish dawn has cracked
We must be on the road again in flight,
In glorious flight, world's record speed to try
On all the roads of Greece, for Canada Dry!"

"Oh, Mickey, can't you stay here more?" cried Clara,
Hot for some consummation with the mouse;
"They say upon the shores of the blue Cari-
Bbean Sea is a pagoda house
Where mice love more than Deirdre did in Tara!
Oh, that I there could shed my milky blouse
And be with you a weekend or a year!"
So saying, she rough-tongued his rounded ear.

"Clara, beware!" cried Minnie. "I'll not let you
So carry on with Mick while I'm alive!
Even if you make him now, he'll soon forget you
When we go speeding off upon our drive
Over the million roads of Greece. Upset you?
Too bad! He's mine! You, just when we arrive,
Start making cow eyes at him. Your tough luck!
Alone with him tonight I'll squeak and fuck!"

11

Meanwhile the brilliant red sun in the sky
Of Western Greece now turned a fiercer pale.
A cook in Athens throws an eggplant pie
Against a restaurant wall; he missed—a nail
Appears now in his forehead where the guy
Named Alfred Funz the pie hit could not fail
To take revenge by shooting it from a pistol
Which shot but nails: its barrel was of crystal,

So that a person near enough could witness
The passage of the nail from end to end
Of the Greek gun, which ended physical fitness
For whomsoever—husband, wife, or friend—
Its missile struck. From manliness to itness
It turned the waiter, caused his knees to bend,
And flung him straight into the *au delà*—
Hard punishment for throwing moussaka!

A meaningless violence seems to plague the world
Which world cannot get rid of. Men debate
In great assemblies, with all flags unfurled,
The cause of peace, go home, and fill with hate
And get their rifles; brows with sweat empearled,
Feeling some insult to their purse or State
Or that some person is too much unlike them—
It's hard to see why that should make them strike them!

Hard punishment for any on this earth
To have to leave it in his early years
Before he's had his soul's and body's worth
Of ecstasy and action! hard for ears
To have their function stunted from one's birth;
Hard for the eyes not to see what appears.
Hard are the changes brought about by violence
And even, sometimes, by some fact of science—

The change, for instance, of a man to glassware
By trocadminium phosphate steriodinus,
A horrible substance scattered on the grass where
Two characters from *Ko*, one fair as Venus,
The other once a coach, in Provence ask where
A picnic place might be, safe from the keenness
Of the wild, whistling Mistral. They are shown
A field, by an old man with head of bone.

These two are Alouette, a Tucson belle,
And Pemmistrek, her lover. They much voyaged
Through Michigan, then o'er the ocean's swell
To vast New Asia, where Alouette encouraged
The tourist trade with an immense hotel,
The Munster Mooson, which was then disparaged
By certain persons as imperialistic,
Which didn't please Alouette, who was a mystic

Of sorts, who thought of love and only that.
The Mooson she had built because a panther
Came to her in a dream and ate her hat,
Then stood up on its hind legs like a dancer,
Then changed to a hotel, all cool and flat.
Next day she brooded; then, "I've got the answer!"
She cried, and started building. When, however,
She heard that version of her deed, she never

Had one day's doubt that she should leave her holdings
To a New Asian outfit, if, of course,
It was all right with Pemmistrek. What foldings
Into his arms, and kissing her with force,
And saying "What, to us, my love, are mouldings,
Are bell boys, elevators, Kleenex, coarse
Americans in short Bermuda pants?
How better far fresh air and high romance!"

They left—she her hotel, he being coach,
And toured New Asia, then to Europe via
The Trans-Siberian Express, steel roach
That runs so far, runs, almost, from Korea
To Aix, where they are now, and now approach
Their deadly destiny. What an idea!
A chemical that makes a person vitreous!
Horrible change, from flesh and blood—and piteous.

On lying down in it, Pemmistrek immediately
Feels an absurd sensation in his thorax,
Stares at his hand and finds it, inconceivably,
Transparent, through which he sees fields of borax,
Light green. Then his whole body glazes evenly,
And he, though conscious, can perform no more acts.
The sun shines down on him, as you'd expect, from
The sky, and shows all colors of the spectrum.

And Alouette, who loved him so, and had
For such a while, seeing him turned to substance
That could not feel nor see, know good from bad,
Nor walk around, nor eat, nor answer questions,
Began to shake, like one who has gone mad
And changed, herself, all tremblings and convulsions,
Into a giant bird—metempsychosis
Due to ornithological neurosis.

One goes along, and one is feeling pleasant
And normal, certainly, and full of life,
When suddenly one feels an effervescent
Sub-epidermic tingle, like a knife,
Then feels stark feathers pushing, one is Desmond
Or Betty Lou no more, no more the wife
Of Doctor Fosgrove of Three Fifty-Two
Hyannis Lane, no more Gentile or Jew

But absolute pure bird—asocial malady,
That frees one from one's culture! Curious case!
It almost always started as an allergy
With a slight hint of feathers round the face—
One ended up like something from mythology
Which guards a hill or other sacred place.
It lasted days, or months, though meditation
Could speed its cure, as could the imitation

Of a bouquet of roses (this is an ancient
Orthodox Jewish ritual which survives
Chiefly in jokes and in one smallish painting
By Pisanello, with beflowered sides:
A young, rose-costumed rabbi with a fainting
Woman in a green wood). Now she decides
To act, at once. "For maybe he can shake
This illness off, or its enchantment break—

I'll fly him to a hospital at once!"
To pick him up is hard, and to transport
Is harder still. Now through the field she runs
To gather weeds, of which she makes the sort
Of basket which balloonists who do stunts
Are fond of leaping out of, or, at court,
Ladies pile plums in for the delectation
Of him or her who rules their sovereign nation.

So Pemmistrek is tied inside the lock
Of twining Provence weeds, and Alouette takes
Him, windowy, to Rome. And there, with shock
And microsurgical laser beam that shakes
His flesh free from the vitreous parent block,
He's cured! He moves—and breathes. Dr. McSnakes,
Who did the work (amazing!), does the best
He can to help Alouette: "Poor child, with breast

Of down, and downcast wing, who overspread
My chair, would that I knew a certain cure
To turn that bird's head to a human head
And give you back your feminine allure—
I would, but I cannot. I can, instead,
Assure you, though, that you will change. The pure
Dry air of Rome this time of year should help
You to come back to womanhood. Eat kelp

And drink a lot of water. Try to find
A synagogue. Your friend will have amnesia.
There is no way a man can keep his mind
Intact when packed in vitreous anaesthesia
As he has just now been. If you are kind,
However, and let him live in love and leisure,
His memory will come back. This morning, though,
It's as if he'd been born an hour ago."

He opened the great window, and they flew
Together over Rome. Then down together
They walked about, and he found nothing new
Or strange about the fact that she was feather
Where he was flesh, or that her legs were blue.
He felt so strange amid that ancient heather
Of Palatine and Capitoline, knowing
The whole of human life within him growing—

Surprised by joy, impatient as the wind,
Full of the amorous passions of a man
And all the careless ease of youth. He grinned.
"Can we be happy here? I think we can.
Dear feathery friend! Oh, were you trunked or finned,
Or both, I'd love you equally!" "My plan,"
Alouette said, "though's to change to girl as soon as
I ever can. It's nicer." Then when noon was

Upon the Palatine, where these two wandered
In happy delectation of a future
That could not be far distant, as they squandered
Sweet words upon each other's tint and feature,
Pemmistrek bumped into a white unlaundered
Rough marble portal faint with architecture,
Which opened, when he touched it, dark and wide,
And he fell in, then closed, he trapped inside.

He fought to open it but fought in vain.
Once in each hundred years that door would budge.
It was designed by Archibald of Spain—
A famous architect who held a grudge
Against Pope Leo Seventh ("The Insane")—
To capture Leo's mistress, Ellen Gudge
Of England, whom he'd meet upon this hill
Each Monday night, in weather warm or chill.

The Spanish builder had slipped a phony note
In Ellen's door, which told her on that night
To wear a big warm fuzzy winter coat
And at their rendezvous turn to the right,
Descend, and at the marble mountain goat
Turn left and press the buzzer with delight
Which she would see in front of her, and enter
The door which opened. When he this had sent her

The guileful Archibald had gone inside
The Roman cave to wait for her. She was
The most, since what time Cleopatra died,
Beautiful creature ever dressed in fuzz,
Which even women never have denied.
And so when Archibaldo heard the buzz
He felt not only vengeance coming to him
But also fire-tipped tremors running through him!

19

Alas! the one who entered was not Ellen,
But a clove-covered steaming Chinese fish
Who picked his bones in whispers. Trojan Helen,
Whether on mountain's top or ancient dish
Adorned with fruit trees you abide, or, dwelling
In some obscure hut, wrinkled, hear my wish:
That no man, filled with passion, feel again
What Archibald of Spain experienced then.

Grant this, and grant no more. The Pope, of course,
Had long ago found out the Spaniard's plan.
He had a thousand spies whom threats of force
Obliged to work incessantly. "The man
Is crazier than I!" With no remorse
The Pope commissioned Papal Chef Wang Fan
To bake a poisoned Chinese walking delicacy
To kill the fool who threatened his fake celibacy.

And so he had. The manner of his killing
Is too repulsive to report. Instead
Let's follow Pemmistrek, who will, God willing,
End up in Finland, where the passage led
The Door had let him into. But that milling
Throng he sees immediately ahead?
Those ocean's waves, that sunlight on his pinky—
Yes, in two minutes he had reached Helsinki!

That cave was built in a mysterious way
And Archibald of Spain had been a genius
Far greater than the greatest of his day.
What puzzles me is that our high school seniors
In science know the work of Ludge, Dubray,
Pistaki, Meyers, Einstein, Fox, Velsenius,
But do not know this master of illusion!
And now a boat sails up with a profusion

Of female beauty on it. "Who are you?"
One lovely cries, attired in open shirt,
With long blonde hair and features almost new.
She was an Early Girl, made from the dirt
Of Western Finland by MacShane Depew,
A wild American chemist who to flirt
Was all he cared about, and he had found
A way to make young women from the ground.

In Western Finland there's a soil called "simma"
Pronounced like Jim plus *a* though with an *s*
Instead of *j* (that is, it isn't "jimma")
Which, with an ounce of water, more or less,
And a dash of white pepper from the Hima-
Layan Mountain States, sends up a Bess,
A Sally, or a Benedetta Croce—
Young beauty to impassion the unstodgy,

The valiant men of earth. More than he needed
He could create, since he had lots of pepper
And plenty of soil, and so Depew proceeded
To send such girls all over, like the skipper
Of this cave-entering boat. The one she greeted
So gaily was unconscious as a kipper:
The speed and force of what had happened to him
Struck all at once and violently threw him.

Were these girls like those girls who grew up from
A babyhood to childhood, adolescence,
And then more perfect state? Were they more dumb?
Shyer? More awkward? Or more full of presence?
And from what culture did they seem to come?
What traits, if any did, betrayed their essence?
Were they more innocent than ordinary
Girls? More giving? More relaxed? More merry?

O strange, sweet girls of whom the chemist thought
Who more than other scientists took pity
On those who live for beauty! But I ought
To hurry now to Rome, that brilliant city,
Where Huddel, who so valiantly has fought
Against the tight embrace of Zacowitti,
The Beljab God of Death who smiles at nothing,
Awoke, and broke out in a high, loud buzzing.

If clarity is what we seek in life,
Then life's a disappointment and a fraud,
For nothing's ever really clear, not wife,
Or home, or work, or people who applaud
The finest work you do. But if a knife-
Like deep sensation worthy of a god
Is what you're after, life can furnish plenty—
Some earlier than, some at, some after twenty.

There is the proud sensation, for example,
Of sinking in the ocean in a car;
Or being thrown against a Gothic temple
By an outrageous omophagic czar—
No one should ever feel that he has ample
Experiences which light him like a star:
Stark naked hens and roosters playing cricket,
And Juno, Mars, and Saturn in a thicket.

Of such events the coming back of Huddel
To life was surely one for many people
Who found the trip to Rome well worth the trouble
Although at times the climate made them feeble.
He gave, to all who watched, the thought that rubble
Itself might take a jog around the steeple
If but its atoms came to that decision;
The pleasure this thought gave banned all derision.

In fact this statue, dear to the enlightened
And ignorant alike, was now betraying
Sure signs of coming back to life, which frightened
Old ladies, so that one could find them praying
In the S.S. *Annunziata* night and
Day: what once had died should be decaying,
Not coming back to breathe the air of Rome
And pinch and kiss its girls and take them home.

Most Romans loved it, though; to them it seemed
That life was good again! And Huddel felt
(He had felt nothing for a while), he dreamed,
Or did whatever, that a rope or belt
Had loosened from around him. He esteemed
The sun was hot but not enough to melt
His form completely; he was still half dead
And rather liked this state. The doubters said,

"You must also suppose that Notre Dame
Will start to dance a jig in La Cité,
That Eiffel Tower will make a grand salaam
To all of Paris' tourists one fine day,
And that the Winged Victory will come
Flying along above our sidewalks grey—
If you believe in all of these events,
Then Huddel redivivus makes good sense!"

Buses, however, emptied every several
Minutes, green and yellow buses filled
With famous tourists—Dr. James McDeverel,
Expert in shoulder transplants; Harmon Schild,
The "buggy doctor," known as Richard Feverel
In Zurich Klinik's Literary Guild;
And hordes of others, leaping from their taxis
In sweaters, jackets, cutaways, and maxis,

In minidresses, cashmeres, rubber suits,
Some laughing, others crying, some with amulets,
Consumptive women and presumptuous brutes,
Miss Ellen Foster Tay of East Los Angeles,
And the Italian army's young recruits,
Looking at Huddel, which so far was thankless:
No arm he raised nor shoulder braced nor torso
Bent in a semicircle toward the Corso.

But now . . . he did! He turned all April blue
(The color of the dry air after rain).
A child cried, "Mother! Look! He's coming to!"
And, sure enough, from vales of No-More-Pain,
No-More-Remorseless-Plans-for-Things-to-Do,
And No-More-Love, No-Justice, No-More-Brain,
Someone was rising there! His fingers flexed,
His eyes shone wide, which earlier had been x'd

By deadly Zacowitti. Huddel leaped
Down from his platform base. He felt so strange
In heart and head and leg and arm, so steeped
In puzzling new vibrations at the change
Of state that had come over him! There beeped
Horns everywhere; as at a rifle range
Shots rang all around; from pure excess of feeling
Men wept and cheered; and temple bells were pealing.

This mad crescendo made a car nearby
And its Italian occupants who'd been
Chasing a rare mysterious butterfly
Which had the power of speech drive over in
Excitement, thinking that the reason why
So many minds had gone into a spin
In Central Rome, with many a helicopter a-
Bove their heads, could but be Lepidoptera

Five Hundred Sixty-Five, the one they sought.
"A butterfly!" their chief, Gorso, imagined
He heard somebody say, and cried, "We ought
To head that way! that crowd there—like a pageant—
They must have found our creature!" Overwrought,
He sped the Fiat in a crazy fashion
And hit poor Huddel, shattering him. To be
Killed twice is to be dead eternally,

They say. We'll see. He fell. Then Rome grew blurry
With deadly thunderclouds. To quit that sky
For shelter now was everybody's worry
Save for the crazy scientists who try
To find their bug amidst the storm, and scurry
All round the place where Huddel's ruins lie.
Then suddenly these ruins, by some force
Triumphant welded, swifter than a horse

And stronger than a lion, leap together
And strike the crazy hunters where they run.
Hit by that hand and nearly dead from weather
They raise their hands for mercy, every one,
Then see before them like a speaking feather
The butterfly they sought with axe and gun:
Five Hundred Sixty-Five, both red and white
Its moving wings, how sure and quick its flight!

"I'm sorry that I can't be staying with you,"
The butterfly observed, "but I'm obliged
To go wherever mercy is at issue.
You know you didn't find me: I arrived
When your survival was so frail a tissue
That if I hadn't come you'd have capsized
Beneath the deadly blow that Huddel gave
And found in Rome an awful, watery grave.

Give up your quest for me. I can't be gotten.
Go be the consolation of the poor;
Convince the man of shame that he's not rotten;
Perfume the harried worker in the sewer;
Bind up the wounds of youth with gauzy cotton;
And make the days of hell on earth be fewer!"
While saying this, Five Hundred Sixty-Five
Stood poised above their heads, as if to dive,

Which then it did. Strange that a creature which
Has neither man's intelligence or feelings
Can hold a view of life that is so rich!
So moths that leap at lightbulbs on our ceilings
So maddeningly that we turn off the switch
To sit in darkness with the apple peelings
And half-filled brandy glasses in the evening
Of summer days might cure us of all grieving

If we could but hear their philosophy.
However, none of them can talk, which is
Why Enzo Gorso and his cohorts free-
Ly gave up love and laughter, bed and bus-
Iness to chase this stunning wingèd flea,
The talking butterfly and moral whiz
Five Hundred Sixty—but you know already
And must be wondering what Huddel, heady

With new-found powerful life, was up to while
These hunters heard a bug philosophizing.
He felt as full of mysteries as the Nile
And felt the strangest force within him rising.
Vowing to live this time in a new style
(More wildly free and much more enterprising)
He turned from those he'd struck, and, turning there,
Finding new strength he rose into the air.

Pursuing what he takes to be a parrot
That calls him by name, Huddel descends
The Valley of the Tiber, while a carrot
Grows up in Houston, and while Pemmistrek's friends,
His new friends, that is, Early Girls, inherit
The job of curing him. "He has the bends!"
Cries one. "But no!" "He's darling!" cries a third.
And Alouette flies, far off, a helpless bird.

If she will find the passage to the snowy
City where her lover is and if
He still will be the Daphnis to her Chloe
If she does not, somehow, de-hippogriff
It's hard to say. Bedazzled by the showy
Beauty of these girls who make him sniff
For losses dim and foggy in his brain,
He goes off with them on a Finnish train.

It takes him to the north of Finland, touted
To be quite fair. He felt he was in love
With Early Ann, and they made love about it.
She was afraid, though—gave an anxious cough,
Looked at him, closed her eyes, wept, smiled, and pouted.
"What's wrong?" he asked. "Was I too rude or rough?
I'm sorry if I was. You made me happy!"
She stood up in her blue and white serapi.

"I-I like you too," she said. "But I'm afraid
Of what may come to be." And as she said it
A strange fine mist exuded from the bed
On which the two had lain like persons wedded.
"I fear it is some city we have made,"
The artificial beauty wept. "I dread it.
The old gnome in the peachtree prophesied it."
Into his arms for comfort then she glided.

"What? City? I don't understand a word,"
Said Pemmistrek. "The prophecy was this,"
Said, brightly, Ann, "that each time it occurred
An Early Girl responded to a kiss
And lay down with the fellow she preferred
And held him to her hard for emphasis,
The double of a city would appear—
A ringer for the chilly real one, beer

Exuding from its barroom taps, and trolleys
Ringing down its urban streets, bananas
Sold by vendors from high carts, and college
Students dreaming up some pure Havanas
Where love would govern all, not francs or dollars,
And alligators in the fake savannas
Of its aquarium or giant zoo—
And many another subtle detail too—

But something would be wrong, some little change
Which made a person wandering there feel crazy
Who thought he was in his true city; strange
Events would make his sense of things grow hazy—
Beds, for example, at the stock exchange.
Sometimes it was just air, which made one lazy,
So that all action had a different rhythm,
As if one had a hippopotamus with him

Who would not move too fast. Sometimes the light
Was what was different. Viewed in solid pink
With polkadots of yellow, Paris might
Be beautiful, but not quite what you'd think;
In such a city one would welcome night,
If night could change those colors, or strong drink."
"How strange it is!" "One love gasp can achieve it!"
Said healthy Pemmistrek, "I don't believe it!"

But, actually, forming at his side
Was Philadelphia, white as the receiver
Of a new "sandal" telephone, the pride
Of Bell's insane inventors, and the savior
Of those with feet which talk. This town was wide
And high and windowed, and no true believer
Could tell it, save for color, from the town
In Pennsylvania, where it settles down;

So that there are two cities right together,
One the old Philadelphia, one the new one.
The new has all bright white or snowy weather,
And it is hard to say which is the true one;
Each smells of rope and roofing, leaf and leather,
And each sends mixed sensations coursing through one.
Each time, good God! that Pemmistrek makes love
Will some new city hit us from above?

The earth in that case will be like an album
Filled up with stamps and no blank spaces showing—
A huge refectory of urban paldom—
And then on top of one another growing
These duplicates would hold the earth in thraldom.
Only the top ones would have sun or snowing,
So most would not be light at all, or airy,
The truth—good news!—is that they're temporary.

Into existence suddenly released,
They'd stay until the sun had done its job
By rising once and setting, then decreased
Until they vanished, causing those to sob
Who like new places. To the west and east
And north almost as far as penguins mob
The crumbs Kaploona empties in the drifts
And south as far, men saw these city shifts,

And, startled by them, often I would guess
Leaped into bed themselves with female citizens
They'd felt too shy with earlier to express
Their passion with such wholesome lack of reticence.
"What? Harold! Why?" "I really love you, Tess!"
So Cracows, Nices, Zurichs, Bombays, Patersons
Inspire what without the control of birth
Will soon exhaust the resources of earth.

O Birth Control! How radiantly superior
You are to Love Control! O arms and legs!
O pelvic threshold! Exquisite interior!
O breasts for which the thirteen-year-old begs
And marvels over when they soon appear to her!
Thigh, calf, and foot! O delicate as eggs,
You, wrists! and face, how can I praise you properly?
Besides, it's all been done by Akopopoli,

Who, though, unfortunately, wrote in Greek,
Which I can't read, so doubtless plagiaristic
Is somewhat of the praise which here I speak.
Still, repetition is characteristic
Of greatest wisdom: what said Christ the meek
Not said before by Prophet or Greek mystic?
He simply put it in a different order.
So Pemmistrek will every day embroider

The planet with new cities. He knew not
What life was like, therefore it seems to him,
Amnesiac, that this strange life he's got
In Finland's snows among the cherubim
Made by MacShane Depew, a heavenly lot
Of love works none would choose to merely skim,
Is Everyman's. Now pausing in his flight
On Samos Huddel lands to spend the night.

I don't believe I made entirely clear
What sort of matter Huddel was composed of
After his second recrudescence here
On earth where men are usually disposed of
Once and once only, even when quite dear
To gods who have the power to change them. Most of
The Greeks the Greek gods saved were made divine,
Not given human life a second time.

In fact, it seems a questionable gift;
One might, I think, like something slightly altered
When one came back from death, the slightest shift,
Something, at any rate, so that what faltered
The first time round would get a little lift
And have more chance to feel itself exalted.
Huddel, indeed, was not the same he once was:
Half flesh, half concrete, flying into sunsets,

He had the strength of seven men; he could
Lift two-ton weights above the people's heads;
His slightest touch would splinter stoutest wood
And he could take the Dodgers and the Reds
And hurl them into center field for good.
But here he was on Samos, and the Feds
Were fearful that if Soviet Russia found him
They'd build a whole new war machine around him.

"Think of him mating with those Soviet maidens!"
Said Arragaw DePew, a slithy G-Man;
"Those Rooskies know just what to do. In cadence
Every hour some new threat to a free man
Would be begun inside the girl he laid ins-
Ide the Birth-Rate Building. Unless we man
A nuclear sub to cut him off at Samos
We may lose everything!" "Te gaudeamus,"

The choirboys sang in Rome, and "Try to find me!"
Stout Huddel sighed, intuiting the project
The American government had. "No one assigned me
To fight for any side. Of life the object
Is to be strong and glad. Three births remind me
That I was meant to live. No sub or prop-jet
Shall force me from this Asiatic sea—
Above all else I prize my liberty!

O Liberty, you are the only word at
Which the heart of man leaps automatically!"
As Huddel spoke, the folk on Samos, stirred at
The way he spoke and what he said, ecstatically
Began to shriek with pleasure. "I prefer dat,"
Said Mugg McDrew, the sub commander. "Practically
Makes dis ting a cinch! We'll just pretend
Dat we're Greeks too, den take our little friend!"

The sub, already there beneath the harbor,
Now opened up, and ten Americans swam
Ashore and started searching for the garb or
Part of garb that, aided by the ham
Inside each one, could help them play the barber,
The farmer, and the chief. They gave a damn,
These gallant boys, enough to risk their all for
A blow against the Reds, more vile than sulphur.

When they are all attired in stolen clothes
And walking through the Samian crowd, which, cheering
Huddel, to the left, then right side flows
Like a Ferrari with a melted steering
Wheel, they see a maiden like a rose
All pink and white toward the temple veering
Where Huddel is declaiming—"Watch out! You
Are being trailed by agents from the blue

Aegean, or whatever sea it is!
They want to trap you, so beware!" Then Huddel,
Glancing around, saw one who fitted his
Idea of a phony Greek—unsubtle
His idiot disguise! He blew a kiss
To his sublime informant, who was trouble
To those who thought to make a capture here,
And struck the fake Achaian with a spear

Which was a part of Hera's holy temple,
Something he obviously should not have done,
For it made all the earth of Samos tremble!
A giant earth- or sea-quake had begun,
Which made the Samians, screaming, disassemble.
An act of sacrilege, the only one
That Huddel ever did, caused this upheaval
Which smashed the classic with the medieval

And smote the Samian robber in his cave
And threw the Samian shepherd from his mount
And shot a thousand dead up from the grave
And broke more water jars than I can count;
And, while the island cracked, a tidal wave
Like a huge copy of *The Sacred Fount*
Smashed everything in sight and then retreated,
Leaving old Samos totally depleted.

Yes, there was nothing on this island now:
No eagles, no bazoukis, no percussion,
No moussaka, no blossoms on the bough
Of the delightful peartree where the buzzing
Of bees made glad the lad who led the cow;
And all the persons who had been discussing
The ways to solve their personal problems are
Gasping at sea and cling to any spar.

Life's simple in such crisis situations,
Provided they don't last for very long:
Such fortitude, such sympathy, such patience,
Such pleasure in a patriotic song!
Too bad that just by decimating nations
One usually has such things. It's wrong.
One ought to live as nobly every minute
As these folks did at sea while struggling in it

To stay afloat and find their island home
Just one more time, and then, they vowed, forever
They'd be obedient to the speechless dome
And parchless eye of heaven; they would never
Do any bad or selfish thing, nor roam
From Samos off to any place whatever.
These vows were heard by no one but the fishes
Whom usually they fried and served on dishes

With lemon on the side, and sometimes rice.
These edibles, though, found incomprehensible
Their human language, which did not suffice
To make the fish do anything more sensible
Than swimming out of earshot. Fish are nice
In being, though we eat them, not revengeful.
I think that we would probably be meaner
To those who washed us down with their retsina!

However, back to Huddel, who was flying
Above the wavetops, seeking the beauty who
Had warned him of the U. S. agents. Spying
Her floating near, he scoops her from the blue
And flies with her to Africa. Now sighing,
Now cursing violently, Mugg McDrew
Cruises the choppy sea in loop-the-loops
To save his Greek-costumed aquatic troops.

He finds them, all but one, a boy named Amos
Frothingham, who, wishing to escape
America's secret service (though it's famous,
To guns he much prefers the girl, the grape,
The peartree and the plough, and so on Samos
Decides to live, and was in such good shape
That he could swim against the tide) had swum
Alone to shore again, but was struck dumb:

For Samos, Samos was not what it was!
A million people jammed its dusty streets!
Construction pierced the ear with hideous buzz!
Enormous libraries, with busts of Keats,
Shelley, and Colonel Pepperidge, sheltered fuzz
Who searched for foreign spies among the treats
That literature offered! Traffic lights
Changed hue, to promise multicolored nights!

What was this transformation of an island
City to a metropolitude?
The taxi and the steam drill pushed the silent
Sea aside and smashed the island's mood!
How could that be? I think a Danish pilot,
With engine trouble, with his parachute
Came down to earth in Finland and so flattered
An Early Girl, so many kisses scattered,

So many a light caress placed here and there,
That she succumbed to him, upshot of which
Was this new form of Samos. What a scare
It put in Amos' bosom! "No such switch
Is possible!" he cried. "It isn't fair!
Just at the moment I decide to ditch
Urban America, it comes back to haunt me!
I'll kill myself! Oh God! Life doesn't want me!"

And, saying this, he ran into the sea
To drown himself—at least, he thought he did,
Thought he was running blindly, terribly
Into the salt sea where nobody lived;
He ran from two till quarter after three,
Stopped, opened up his eyes, and saw what gift
His life had given him: the old, true, empty
But beautiful Samos, at whose harbor entry

The Samian citizenry now climbed ashore.
The tide had changed for which they thanked the goddess
And vowed that none would violate ever more
Her sanctuary. Meanwhile in Nevada's
Gambling halls, the odds are five to four
That Mickey Mouse will conquer the White Protes-
Tant Anglo-Saxon rats who are his rivals.
The mice, both he and she, are better drivers,

The gamblers say; and many a bet is made
By those who can't afford it, kids in sneakers
With wistful looks, who all night long have prayed
For Disney's two to win this crazy Preakness
Through all the roads of Hellas. Undismayed,
Terence and Alma Rat have shown no weakness,
But, driving just as fast, with less support,
Intend to win. In Athens, in Earls Court,

And in the drowsy empires of the East
Interest is high, and television offers
Daily two-hour reports, a visual feast
To all who love the contest. Mickey proffers
A candy bar to Minnie. "Brewer's Yeast
Is all I'll eat today," squeaks she, but softens
And takes the bar and takes a bite. "My diet
Is less to me than keeping Mickey quiet

In mind and heart so he can be victorious,"
She thinks—while Donald in the back seat's dozing
As they pass Delphi, famous for its oracles,
Descend to Thrakis, famed for early closing,
Then speed with trembling wheels to Crete the glorious
Across the "Bridge of Spray," made by the hosing
Of people on the islands on the way;
This would not work in San Francisco Bay

Because there are no islands there to hold
The people spurting water; but there are
So many isles (twelve thousand five, all told)
Of Greece, there was no problem; so the car,
Supported by this water brave and cold,
Could brightly beam along, a daytime star,
Bearing two noted mice of black and one
Of yellow duck, whose name, you know, was Don.

O Donald Duck, if ever you could know
The destiny that waits for you in Crete
You'd urge your best friend Mickey to go slow
And exercise the webbing on your feet
To leap into the blue sea air, for though
Your life with him and Minnie seems complete
Soon a most horrible wedge will drive between
You and your friends. Meanwhile the beckoning green

Of fair Heraklion with its Labyrinth
Spoke to them from afar. "Land, land at last!"
Said Mickey. Minnie said, "And it's a cinch
We'll all be glad this watery ride is past,
Although it was exciting!" "May the tenth:
Two thousand miles—eight hours." Don smiled and laughed
Then passed the book to Minnie: "Let Terence Rat
Just try to beat or even compete with that!"

And Donald's doom was on him in two days . . .
A Chinese gentleman named Hu Ching Po
Was interested in living different ways:
Spending the month on Crete, he wished to know
The black, the white, the intervening greys
Of all that happened there. Well, he was so
Surprised to see a duck walk up and speak
To him that he stared madly at its beak—

Or "bill"—men have a lot of names for noses:
"Schnozzola," "target," "ray-gun," and "proboscis";
And "implement for getting kicks from roses,"
Or "helpful, with the eyes, in winning Oscars,"
And "fresh air opens up what clothespin closes."
Whether by cows or beautiful young Toscas
Borne in the midst of face, it has the beauty
Of being both delicate and heavy-duty:

We breathe all day and then we breathe all night—
Sometimes, it's true, the mouth takes over for it,
But mainly it's the nose, when sun shines bright
Or when stars gleam, that does, like Little Dorritt,
More than it seems it ought to do. Our sight
Is veiled by lids, our hands in sleep lie forward
And do not touch, our ears the brain takes care of
By making dreams of sounds we're not aware of—

But nose, you go on breathing all night long!
What was I speaking of? Oh, Donald's bill.
Yes, well, an animal, chicken or King Kong,
Will have a different nose than humans will.
A nose which on a girl might look all wrong
Would on a hen be beautiful; yet still
We think our own of a superior grade.
Don's was two dots upon a bony blade.

When Hu Ching Po, astonished, saw the beak
Of Donald Duck, and heard him talk, he couldn't
Believe he'd not gone crazy. In a week
They had him out of surgery, a wooden
Brain inside his head, and in his cheek
A "thinking cathode," which would help him goodn-
Ess knows get through life's ordinary duties.
But now to Mickey and his "You, too, Brutus"

Attitude toward Donald, for he found him
In Minnie's arms, with Minnie gently sighing!
"Minnie, goddamn, you've your two arms around him!
I see," cried Mick, "a duck will soon be dying!"
And, seizing a huge rock, began to pound him
(Poor Donald Duck) to death. "I'm not denying
I hugged him hard, but good Lord, Mickey, listen!"
He stopped; he saw her eyes with teardrops glisten.

45

"Donald—I hope he's not dead yet—poor Donald—
Oh, Mickey, see, he's breathing! yes!" "Come, tell me!"
The barely pacified Mickey cried, "I've coddled
This duck enough! Don't try to overwhelm me
With sighs and tears. Goddamn, I feel dishonored!
What consolation are you trying to sell me?"
"Oh!" Minnie said; then, with a voice like bells,
"He was upset at hurting someone else.

It was the kind of thing we've gone through too—
Don't you remember, Mickey? Oh, you must!
Before the world got used to me and you.
Staring at my small shapely mousy bust
Full many a mariner would go cuckoo;
And you, you were not unaware, I trust,
How many of those who heard you speak your name
Went totally and hopelessly insane.

You know there is a hospital in Switzerland
With two pavilions, Mickey and Minnie Mouse,
For crazy people who go round insisting that
Rats and mice can speak. This crazyhouse
Has services and doctors both most excellent,
Yet no one's ever left it cured." A louse
Leaped through the air toward Mickey's ear but missed it.
Minnie took Mick's left hand in hers and kissed it—

Or, rather, kissed his white four-fingered glove
(These mice have clothing on their hands all year).
"Well, Donald drove one mad today. Oh, love,
Forgive him. And me, too. He felt such fear . . .
I was but pitying him." She kneeled. Above
Her head her lover gave her the all-clear
By making spring-like signs of benediction.
Then both went over to Donald. "His condition

Is grave," said Mickey. "He may really die.
We've got to find a top-flight veterinarian,
And soon!" As through Heraklion's streets they hie,
Let's turn to Huddel and the lovely airy in-
Spiring girl he's found and holds, who fly
Above that substance held by the Aquarian
To Africa, where roams the wild rhinoceros,
That angry brute, and the mild hippopotamus.

Landing in Kenya, girt about by huts,
This pair have scarcely time to greet each other
Or even see each other when there juts
Into the side of each of them a rather
Tremendous deadly spear. "No ifs or buts,"
Thinks Huddel, "life means not to give me breather!"
"What are you doing here?" the natives cry.
"What are you? Are you man? How can you fly?"

Huddel at once sensed he had an advantage
In being strange to them and seeming magic
But tried to tell the truth. "In the Atlantic
An island lies, hight England, known for tragic
Theatre, hot tea, and great Romantic
Poetry. It's hard to find an adjec-
Tive to describe it all!" "Speed up," they said,
"Or ere your story's finished you'll be dead!"

"Well, I am from that island," Huddel moaned,
Pretending suddenly he felt the anguish
Of being far from it. He fell, and groaned.
"What's wrong?" the natives cried, no longer angry
So much as curious. "Perhaps he's stoned,"
One young spear-bearer said, in secret language—
For drug use in the village was quite frequent
And had its own patois. Just then an egret

Flew over Huddel, and he suddenly rose
Grasping sweet Aqua Puncture in his arms
(That was her name) to join that bird. Her clothes
Flew all about, and all beheld her charms
Spellbound, while Huddel in the airstream goes
One hundred miles an hour. Black alarms
Sent up in smoke through Kenya are too tardy
To catch that thrice-born aeronaut so hardy.

Hardy as a Venetian gondolier
When moving slim black boat against the tide;
Hardy as Greek or Trojan charioteer
When war's concussions cast his steeds aside;
Hardy as these and more, and full of cheer,
Huddel once more descends from his sky ride,
This time in Tropical China, a peculiar
African region very like to fool you.

For everyone who lived there was Chinese!
And all the buildings there were Chinese too!
The women wore their skirts slit at the knees!
Some older men resembled Fu Man Chu!
And there were paper lanterns in the trees.
Perhaps it all was caused by you know who,
An Early Girl, caught in the coils of passion;
Or maybe it was made in Papend fashion—

That is, perhaps created by the fancy
Of one ambitious man, to soothe his soul.
Perhaps an old monk skilled in necromancy
Had seen the whole thing on an ancient scroll
And worked, to please his young assistant Nancy
Chang, to make it real and make it whole.
Whatever cause there was for this phenomenon
It amazed Huddel and his belle companion.

They landed, this time, luckily, out of sight
Of the inhabitants, so they had a moment
To look around a bit and gauge their plight.
The people's manners seemed like a good omen:
Everyone was exceedingly polite.
"In such a place as this," said Huddel, "no man
Should do us wrong. Let's see if we can dodge
The carts and crowds and find someplace to lodge."

Aqua, it happened, spoke Italian, which
The people understood, for Tropical China
Belonged to Italy from nineteen six
Till the end of World War Two; and some old-timers
Recalled that epoch with nostalgic twitch
As Bellay France, and Foster Carolina,
Or baby thinking of its mother's breast:
"No doubt about it, that time was the best!"

For Italy had brought a certain order
To Tropical China which it had not had,
And unlike all the countries on its border
Each night its jungly Chinese streets were glad
With sounds of mandolin, flute, and recorder:
Vivaldi then competed with the sad
And Neapolitan songs; here flirted Tosca;
There Norma died; here Pu Tang Fong ate pasta,

While toucans called and monkeys leaped around
And crocodiles went sliding down the river;
The feetchekee bird made a looping sound,
And jungle night at last, that Indian giver,
Took itself off or changed to day: one found
That chilly morn had come and with a shiver
Returned to one's pagoda in the brush,
And then the sun rose with a velvet hush!

They found a lodging, as they'd hoped they would,
A straw pagoda, and they had a chance
To get to know each other. It was good
To hear the gongs and tarantella dance
And merely sit there at their table's wood
And gaze—for the beginnings of romance
Are often very quiet, like a sailor
Drowned in the sea, or like a power failure—

Or rather, its results: no songs, no speeches,
Nothing but stilly silence in the air.
One could have heard the fuzz grow on the peaches
If there had been no one but those two there.
Then finally they spoke. "Experience teaches,"
Said Huddel, "that to find someone you care
A lot about is life's supreme event.
Tell me about you—are you heaven-sent?

Did you descend to Samos from the clouds,
A messenger from Zeus or from Athena?
Or did you make your way through Samian crowds
From powerful Poseidon's wet arena?
Or are you of those mortals doomed to shrouds
Brought back to lovely life by a novena?
Are you love's pattern? or love's syllable?
Whether you are of this or that race, tell—

For I don't know exactly what *I* am:
I have been born three times." Aqua responded,
"I know about your life. An anagram
On an old jar told much, and then, beyond that,
I read about you in the Amsterdam
Gazeeter on the same day I absconded
From the Antiquities Museet. John Ruskin
Was my great-grandfather. I am Etruscan.

Unknown to other folk our leaders had
Worked out a way of keeping men alive—
And women, obviously," she smiled. "Too bad
There wasn't time to save at least, say, five—
Just one. What would, I thought, make me most glad
Would be to see more like myself survive,
But that was then. Now here in this pagoda
Is all I want!" She kissed him for a coda.

And outside they were celebrating Easter
In African Chinese Italian style.
Inside those two embraced. When he released her,
Huddel said, "Let's go out there for a while
To join our joy with theirs in this great feast for
A man come back to life, as I did. Smile.
What's wrong? You're looking worried." She said, "Well,
I am, a little. But—I'll come." The bell

Was sounding Paternosters à la Chang
With Verdian riffs and Congo syncopations,
When from the straw pagoda's door there sprang
These two caught in the enmity of nations.
They joined the streaming multitude and sang
A song of love and youth and their elations—
Unfortunately, staring at them through
A nearby window's straw was Mugg McDrew!

If you are wondering about Aqua's age,
Since she is young and gorgeous, though Etruscan,
And how she got her name, don't skip this page.
Her grandmother had terrified John Ruskin
By talking to him, while the English sage
Was studying her. What is a man to trust in?
He trusted in his feelings—pounding heart!
She was alive, and not a work of art.

Frightened at first, Ruskin became enchanted
With this Etruscan beauty and her story:
Here was, at last, Etruria, not invented
By dry historians, but real. Before, he
Thought history hardly real at all. He wanted
To spend his life with her! She made his glory
But died in childbirth near the Coliseum.
Their daughter was confined in a museum

By envious archaeologists who stole
Her from John Ruskin's carriage at the border—
This loss almost deprived him of his soul!
He'd see his child in dreams, start walking toward her
Then suddenly find himself upon the Mole
In Venice. So she would obey each order;
The archaeologists stuck in her veins
A needle that exempted her from pains

And bodily movement yet which let her grow.
She bloomed apace. Nor did John Ruskin ever
Discover it was she. Why should he go
To Amsterdam or any place whatever
Save Italy? He thought her dead, and so
He stayed, to pour his heart out like a river,
Spending the hours left him, not on tennis
Or careless love, but on *The Stones of Venice*.

(That book! the most important ever penned
For Papend and his helpers! All the while
They built their Andean Venice they would spend
Each night stirred and inspired by its style.)
But now to bring our story to an end
Of Aqua's mother—she stayed in the vile
Etruscan Room of Amsterdamsk Museet
Till one day something happened, which is sweet

To tell of and was sweet for her. The venom
Which had been fed into her veins by those
Who valued stone girls more than girls in denim
And taffeta, wore off, and, like a rose
In the first dawny breeze, near the anemon-
E, her sweet sister flower, in pleasant pose,
She gave a slight, slight shiver and a shake,
Which caused a man to cry, "Am I awake?"

It was the great physician Nyog Papendes,
Commander Papend's father—I am aware
That such coincidences do not lend ease
To readers having perfect faith, but where
The truth is, we must follow. And the Andes'
Doubled Italian city past compare
For love and beauty's founder's father was
The man who saw this scene and felt this buzz

Of love and disbelief. For he had fallen
Quite hopelessly in love with this antiquity,
Or so he thought her, till against the wall in
A state of shock and joy, he felt his rickety
Conventions all collapse around him. Call in
The greatest living experts in propinquity
And they will not find any two made gladder
By being close than these two—or, soon, sadder

At being close no more. He in the ecstasy
Of that first moment, took her in his arms
And cried, "I have so longed to have you next to me
That I cannot believe this: from what Farms
Of Fantasy or Causeways of Complexity
Have you been now transformed into what warms
Me more than high volcano or deep furnace?"
She sighed, "It is a warmth that cannot burn us!

Oh, take me, love, with you. For I have been
A prisoner in this place so long. And I
Have watched you watching me, which was no sin,
I dearly hope, and hoped before the sky
Would turn to changeful April once again
That we could be together." So they fly,
These two, the dark museum, and two years
Live in a blaze of bliss, and there appears

56

As product and summation of their love
A beautiful baby girl, who when a tidal
Wave killed both of her parents, being of
Etruscan heritage, was doped with Mydol
And then some stronger syrop, with a shove
Of needle against her arm. And the recital
Of her life, then, is like her mother's: she
Came back to lively motion suddenly.

Her name she'd simply taken from the first
Sounds she heard spoken when she had awakened
And felt her senses tingle. Someone burst
Into her part of the museum shaken
By bitter news and, happily, had not cursed
But cried out, "Acupuncture! they have taken
Her to the Chinese clinic!" She thought, "Oh!
That's me!" and felt her face with pleasure glow.

Then she had run away, hid on a boat,
And gone to Samos, where brave Huddel found her.
Meanwhile in Pucci-styled white llama coat
Half-brother Papend leans upon a counter
And thinks it is a sadly jarring note
In his sweet life, to have not been around her,
His sister, who, a girl saw in her crystal,
Was once again in life. "If but my sister will

Come here, how good for me! I'll seek her out
And speak to her and try to help her manage
The difficulties, which, I have no doubt,
Beset her in a world she must find savage
And most bewildering." He strolled about
Downing full many a glass of Andean vintage
And smiled. "No one can try to find her better—
I'll send out bird and person, wire and letter!"

McDrew knew where she was! For he had followed
Where Huddel flew. He'd left his submarine,
For it was useless baggage, and had collared
A Tracking Helicopter Five Sixteen
Four Hundred and had flown to China hollowed
Out in the midst of Africa. "I mean
To end this matter here!" he cried. "A shame
That I must kill them both, but that's the game

Free life depends on!" Slipping from the doorway
Of his pagoda as the happy pair
Joined in the mingling throng, he saw the shore, way
Down upon his left, and signaled there
With a "Dark Daylight" Lamp, which had a four-way
Beam control—Torch, Sunlight, Sweep, and Flare—
Each type of beam in different cases relevant.
Mugg used the Sweep, and when he did an elephant

Of green transparent plastic raised its trunk
Above the shore and aimed a deadly dart
At Aqua, gauged to turn her into junk
If it attained her flesh in any part.
Signaled by "Sweep of Daylight" Lamps, such sunk-
En weaponry arises. Oh, the art
We waste upon ingenious ways of killing!
When we were babies, just to be was thrilling—

To hold a rattle up, to eat our mommies,
To learn to walk. Then came our childhood pleasures—
Our baseballs, footballs, rag dolls, origamis.
Next, adolescence, with its sexual treasures—
Who then was thinking about killing Commies?
I just wanted to peek under your feathers
At Aaron's costume party, Ellen White,
And think of you and phone you every night

And swim with you sometimes in Karen's cool
Light-blue piscine, and kiss you cold and dripping
And hold you in my arms. Oh, why not pool
The intellect of all to make one gripping,
Inevitable, bright, ecstatic school
Whose aim will be to keep such times from slipping
Away from us, so that we'd keep so much
Of happiness from weather, mood, and touch

That we'd be generous of our condition
And give it freely, not be always fighting
Those who we fear may threaten our position—
Like Mugg McDrew, who stands here just delighting
In Aqua's almost certain demolition.
Till such school starts, I know a Mouth, which, biting
The heads off such as he, at least could clear
Some space and time for us to found it here.

This Mouth is part of Akitu mythology,
A creed unknown to most men of the West
But treasured by some experts in psychology
As showing the fear of being eaten best
Of all the earth's religions. No apology
Or prayer will work when comes the Mouth, obsessed
With biting. I must find a way to speak
To this tremendous mouth, or bill, or beak.

It's dangerous, though. I wonder. Mugg, meanwhile,
Stands hatefully amidst the world of men
And women, with a slow, unpleasant smile,
Unmindful of a nearby lions' den,
From which three quick young lions—full of guile,
Nobility, and power—out of ten
Come leaping out, feline, immense, and naked,
Rush to the plastic elephant and break it!

Aqua is saved, the deadly dart it had
Intended for the lovely young Etruscan
Held in its trunk, unsent! McDrew, gone mad
In his frustrated wait for the concussion
Of poison dart and girl, picks up a shad
Seen lying on a fish-store plank and throws it
In fury at the slowly moving pair.
Huddel swerves round and grabs him by the hair.

"Damn you! Who are you? Why'd you throw that fish?
'American commander?' What the hell!
You followed me from Samos! Boy, you'll wish
You never joined the service! Ring out, bell,
And hide his screams!" But, with a savage *swish*,
The lions rushed and took him, like a shell
The ocean takes, from Huddel's hands, and left
Him staring, as if of all sense bereft.

These lions were the agents of a man
Who lived inside the jungle and intended
To rescue people, if he could, and plan
To save the world, afraid all would be ended
If humans had their way. This fellow, Dan
McGillicuddy, one day had befriended
A lion in the Hyde Park Zoo. These two
Had planned and plotted then what they must do.

61

Dan thought it wrong that lions should be kept
In iron cages, and he also thought
He'd like a lion's life himself. He slept
In beds but dreamed of caverns; he was caught
In London's civilization, and he wept
To think of freedom in the wilds. He bought
A ticket for himself to Tropical China
And smuggled Beano on the ocean liner

(That was the lion's name) locked in a trunk.
Installed now in the jungle for three years,
Dan had ten lions in his charge, a monk
Of sorts, who gave his life to calming fears,
To rescuing all who might be pierced or shrunk
Or poisoned. People, wiping off their tears,
Would seek to thank him with large sums of money,
But he said no, which many thought was funny.

In any case, these lions then had brought
A body to the cave where they all dwelled.
"What sort of poor sad man is this?" Dan thought,
Then looked at Mugg's insignia—it spelled
"American Secret Service." "What's God wrought?"
He said; "I'm not too fond of this!" but held
Mugg's wrist to take his pulse, then let his lions
Revive him with their animal medical science

Which operated like the tide-flung leaves
Which, covering, in the fall at Vallambrosa,
The swollen stream, give to the heart that grieves
Small room to grieve in fact; and on Formosa
The wheat was being "set to bed" in sheaves,
A drying process thought by Saragossa
To be the most effective that there was.
McDrew revives, and hears a high, loud buzz.

It was the buzz that people said they heard
The first time Huddel took his second breath,
i.e. revived, in Rome. McDrew was stirred
With thoughts of going after him, but death
Now brightly intervened. Not life deferred,
But actual real and everlasting death,
Unrecognizable and terrible death,
Decay of body, dissolution, death.

McDrew had scarcely been prepared for death:
He'd heard that there was such a thing but felt
It was for others. Now the face of death
Appeared to him and he began to melt;
Within five days he was a cask of death—
All bone, no flesh to cling to it like felt,
And tell the brain the lovely things it felt;
He lay upon the cave grass green as felt—

63

For this was death; and Dan McGillicuddy
Bewildered by the failure in this case
Of animal medicine to cure the body
Of Mugg McDrew about the cave did pace
And didn't want to talk to anybody.
The Canton *Star*'s reporter in that place
Pursued him day and night, but Dan said merely
It was a case he'd not as yet seen clearly.

He had not seen a tiny light-green insect
Escaping from the heart of Mugg McDrew
Just as he died. Its power was extrinsic
To anything the jungle savior knew.
The Boboli Gardens held the secret: rinsing
Her hair there a young girl with eyes of blue
Reveals it all to a TienTsin reporter:
"When Mugg was young he was a good deal shorter

(How do I know all this? Our families were
Quite close back home in Akron); he would beg
For anything to make him taller"—her
Eyes lowered here—"he loved me"—swung her leg,
Resumed: "One day a man named Doctor Burr
Said he could offer him a certain egg
For fifteen thousand dollars, but that never
Should he go in the jungle, for whatever

Imaginable reason, for the damp
Of jungle days would cause the egg to hatch
And then, instead of lighting like a lamp
His own impulse to growth, it would unlatch
The life inside itself, first cause a cramp
And then cause death. Say, have you got a match?"
The lovely girl requested. When the TienTsin
Reporter bent to see, she ran off dancing

And screaming horrible threats into the air,
"We'll kill you all, we bugs! Ha ha! Forget it!
You'll never stand a chance!" No underwear!
She rose into the sky. "What have I said? It
Was only so I'd understand!" "Beware!"
She rising cried. She saw a bird and met it
With sloppy kiss. "We cure at first but then
We do our fated work: death to all men!"

While this reporter stood in great amazement
(Until he ran to phone his story in,
For which the poor man was put out to graze with
These words, "You have been drinking too much gin
Or vodka on the job. It's out of phase with
A real reporter's duties: it's a sin
To lie about a true, important story:
Life as it is is the reporter's glory!"

And so the world did not find out the truth
Of what Meralda said until much later,
When "insect eyes" were decimating youth;
Then Pong became a noted commentator
Until he felt the praying mantis' tooth
Which made his life reverse, till incubator
Held all of him there was; then he began
Again to grow and so become a man).

In any case as he was standing facing
The sky amid that dry place full of fountains
And with an eye incredulous was tracing
The young girl's disappearing in the mountains,
While he stood there, poor beaked Alouette was pacing
Outside the Palatine cave, with dreamy countenance.
Touched by some unknown impulse then, she rushed
Into a cab, aside the driver brushed,

And with her wings and claws sped the blue vehicle
To Rome's first synagogue, La Mamma Aleph.
Arriving, she flew out, and knocked the pickle
From someone's hand just entering that palace.
Apologizing, she bumped into a beagle
Who started barking frenziedly. "No malice!"
She sang, then flew inside down to the altar.
"Help me!" she said. "Oh, heaven, if the fault were

My own that I'm a bird I would accept
This cruel fate, but since I know of nothing
That I have done of ill in life except,
Perhaps, construct the Mooson—yet that one thing
I soon abandoned—" here she paused and wept,
While rabbis creeping toward her with black bunting
Prepared to make a fast attempt to net her;
"If I," she sobbed, "were evil, I'd know better

What sense this made . . ." Just then, one rabbi gave
The signals clear: "Five hundred, seven, forty!"
Then flew the crepe, that symbol of the grave!
And one young playful rabbi, Ben Ayorti,
Began to do his "imitations." "Save
The best for last!" cries one who's known as "Shorty,"
"Your imitation of a rose bouquet!"
Hearing this Alouette shivered where she lay

Upon the synagogue's marble floor, although
She did not know the cause. They tied her down
And sent one of their number out to go
And find a truck to drive her through the town
And set her down beside the Tiber's flow
Sufficient miles away. But first the clown
Ayorti does his crazy imitation
And Alouette feels an absurd sensation!

"Help! Let me out!" She has become a woman
Of beautiful form once more. "What was that noise?"
Asks Rabbi Joe; "it sounded really human!"
They lift the crepe and wish that they were boys
Again, and had not chosen to be Roman
Rabbis, but to live for sensual joys—
For Alouette, more dazzling than before,
Lies warm and naked on their temple floor.

Oh for the brush of Rembrandt to depict
The measure of surprise on all these faces!
But Alouette leaped up suddenly and tricked
The crepe around her: she was going places!
She ran outside to where the taxi ticked,
Its driver still unconscious with amazement,
And drove it to the Palatine, but still
Found no trace of her lover on that hill.

How she will ever track him down I can't
Imagine. Feeling awful, she decides
To do what people often do when scant
The hope of help from action, and imbibes
A red Campari soda, which an ant
Imbued with magic information finds
Just as she drinks it down. At once she knows
Where Pemmistrek is, and to the airport goes.

What, although she does know of his amnesia,
She'll feel about his amorousness with
The Early Girls, imagining I'll leave you
For now, and go to Mickey Mouse—and death.
For Donald died. His grave bedecked with freesia
His mouse companions walk away from. "Fifth
To die of those we know: first, Harry Horse,
By measles swept away, and then, by force,

In the Chicago riots, Ethan Mouse;
Then Penny Pig in childbirth; John the Emmett
Burned by a magic lantern." Gabby Grouse
Has flown to be with them in this dilemma t-
O do what all he can, but sorrow plows
Deep grooves in all their faces. At the limit
Of guilt and anguish, Mickey El Raton
(His Spanish name) says, "I cannot go on!

Minnie, if you and Gabby have the heart
To finish up the race, go on and do it.
Me, I feel burned in every mortal part;
I can't do anything, I can't go through it.
But you are free. Here, take the keys and start
The Packard up. I'd hate to think we blew it
Because of what I did and felt!" Her tears
Assured him she would share these lonely years,

These mournful years with him. Gabby said, "Well,
Well, yes, all right, I'll do it, but alone!"
And did heroically. But he fell
From Caesar's cliff. The Packard hit a stone
And leaped to ruin. He hit a church bell
Two miles below, which made a curious tone.
He lost his human powers but was well-met;
The kindly vicar kept him as a pet;

And until London floats in Chios' bay
And Big Ben tolls to passing lobster seekers
And brilliant light is lapped in London grey
He will remain a common grouse, whose features
Are lighted not by reason but by day
Alone. As for the celebrated creatures
He'd left on Crete, they sought a mountain village
To work as common laborers until age

Would whiten them all over. But their dreams
Could not be realized. The daisied slopes
Of Minos' realm grew rowdy with the screams
Of journalists and tourists, and their hopes
Were doomed, they knew it, once the gaudy beams
Of world publicity, like telescopes,
Had found them. "Minnie," Mickey said, "we must
Be gone from here!" She brushed away the dust

That running down the Cretan road to shun
Some crazed photographers had sprinkled over
Her mousy garments all, and cried, "There's one,
Perhaps one way!" "What is it?" Mickey drove her
To where they took the plane to Washington,
Where, in a building dear to Smoky Stover,
They were transformed from living things to comics
By a new drug, which flattened legs and stomachs

And flattened arms and faces, though the eyes
Are left with bright expressions, and the lips
Still curve in two-dimensional surprise
At what this new life offers. Minnie's hips
Are sensuous still, though of a smaller size
Than those with which mouse gloves once came to grips.
King Features' famous doctor, Georges La Berle,
Did this in part to please a certain girl

Who loved new funnies. So, they've looked at us
When we've picked up a newspaper that carries
Their new adventures. On a train or bus,
Going to school, at home, or picking berries,
Quarreling, loving, making such a fuss,
Their lives go on in print from Nome to Paris,
Where nobody can get to them, just read them,
Not touch them, get an interview, or feed them.

Meanwhile, on Samos racing, at the wheel
Is Amos Frothingham. He's found a plot
For taking over Greece, which he, a real
Greek patriot by now, resents a lot.
Added to what most native Greeks would feel
Is his conversion's fire, which they have not.
At the Archbishop Bastilokiokos'
S Palace he gets out and picks a crocus

Inside which is a bug that stings him hard
(One of Meralda's killers? What a horror!)
Which he ignores and slaps it off, and, barred
At first from going in, goes by the barrer
By showing him his Secret Service Card—
Then to Bastilokiokos, mighty warrior
For Hellenism, his head and shoulders bulging
With energy, to him the plot divulging.

On hearing which, the Prelate smacked his blotter
Hard with one hand, picked up the phone, and said
"Bring Postiopos to me!" "Glass of water,
I beg of you!" sighed Amos, then was dead.
The crocus insect was Meralda's daughter
Whose bite was lethal if she bit your head.
So Amos's work was done. They give a feast.
"Here was one good American, at least,"

Wet-eyed Bastilokiokos sadly says
Above the body—"all we most have treasured
In our imagining of the U.S.!
Delightful generosity unmeasured
And free to all, a spirit which said Yes
To what was Greek, found its own land a desert
Because of lack of liberty!" And there
They built a statue in sweet Samos air

Of Amos, who had lost his life while serving
Democracy and Hellas! From the prow
Of ships the world shall see him in the curving
Of Samian marble—none shall make him bow
Or compromise, or aught be but unswerving.
And whosoever wakes on Samos now
May be by him inspired. Let us, however,
Seek out soft African Tropical Chinese weather

Of brand-new spring. Aqua says, "Let us hurry—"
(And caroling natives round about them sung)
"And we can see the Easter Service. Murray
Fitzgibbon writes that when the Cross is hung
From the high bamboo altar, tons of curry
Flow out of Mount Kabogo mixed with dung."
She handed him the guidebook. "Here it is."
He smiled. "How great!" They hugged and had a kiss,

Then ran to the cathedral quickly as
They could. The crowd was vast and oriental—
Ying Pu has more brocade than Yeng Pu has,
But both have quite a lot; and banjo rental
Was doing quite a business on the grass.
"Like England," Huddel thought, once sentimental,
Twice burned, for as he entered the cathedral
A giant pygmy stuck him with a needle.

"For Hengland!" cried the pygmy then, and vanished,
While Huddel slumps on the cathedral floor.
These pygmies from that country had been banished—
One was not used to see them any more.
But sometimes they disguised themselves as Spanish
Marines and sought the "freedom of the shore."
They made themselves look taller with the help
Of special "sea shoes" stuffed with sand and kelp.

Huddel ran out into the crowd but lost
The pygmy in it. "When will we be free,
Sweet Aqua, of such persecution, tossed
Upon a sea of terror such as we
Have no way merited? Perhaps the frost
Of Arctic zones would give to you and me
The kind of private joy we both deserve!"
"Yes. Take me!" To Helsinki then they curve

And with no middle flight. So high they soar
That clouds are far beneath them, and the vapors
Invisible from earth. They spy a shore
Of softest white where little winds play capers
And have the thought to settle there. Why more
Reside on earth, where just to read the papers
Each morning makes one almost give up hope?
This shore was white as sparkling Ivory soap

But Huddel found no solid part, and she
Who flew with him said, "Dearest, what of nourishment?"
"Skylark is good," said Huddel, "and it's free!
And over there, look! in that cloud, that blurrish one,
Je crois qu'il y a légumes des cieux!" Why he
Began to speak in French, to the discouragement
Of all who do not know that language, I
Have no idea, but vegetables of sky

Indeed there were: cloud parsley, heaven's beet
Celestial rutabaga, wind tomatoes,
Gale cucumbers that grow at heaven's feet,
Au delà carrots, spirit world potatoes,
And other produce nurtured by the heat
Of cloudless sun. Sometimes in the Barbados
One has days such as here were all the time;
And sportsmen after a long mountain climb

75

May glimpse a moment of the sweet, pure grandeur
That Huddel and Aqua both now felt pervade them.
You may walk into cafes and command your
Cognac and coffee, but the man who made them,
That billionaire who might not understand your
Problems in the slightest, he would trade them
His cognac industry and his plantations
Could he be guaranteed but these sensations

Which Huddel and his Etruscan girl were feeling.
Sometimes a person, billionaire or hobo,
Will see a young girl caught twixt floor and ceiling
Or on Lake Leman in a sparkling rowboat
And think, "Ah, she's the one, who, by unsealing
The strongest feelings in me, strong as cobalt
Bombs in chain reactions, will enable
Me to rise up above the highest table

In trigonometry or logarithms
And find the free joy that I seek, at last!"
Then, by loud vows or jewels bright with prisms,
Each wins the girl and binds her to him fast;
At happy best, afloat with paroxysms
After the act, the world seems cool and vast—
These instants, though, are hedged by daily living,
Which gets us at the same time it is giving.

So that one often feels hemmed in in spite
Of having one's desire; and then one sees
Another girl upon another night.
One's head is stirred by the cool cafe breeze;
It is not serious, one is not bright,
But yet it seems if one could take *her* knees
Between one's hands and kiss them, one would find
The true and vast space of one's secret mind!

And so one carries on, as Kierkegaard
Describes in *Either/Or* (that's the right title
As I remember, though I find it hard
To get things right when rushed by the recital
Of new events continually! Pard-
On me, then, if I'm wrong), with what is vital
Being a thing continually sought for—
At death it's this that we have come to naught for!

This airy place where Huddel was with Aqua
Gave these sensations every single minute—
So mourners walking down the Via Sacra
See their love's grave and feel they're buried in it
Themselves, they feel their loss with such alacri-
Ty. Goodbye to lobster and to linnet—
Their very being's caught! So this fresh air
Caught their two souls, as if it caught their hair.

II

After a two-year interval, in fact
It's almost three, once more I come, dear Muse,
To write this work, and hope it's still intact,
And you will generously not refuse
Your sweet assistance—which I haven't lacked
At all till now, but had—that I may fuse
What's in my mind and what is in the spectrum
Of earth outside with my typewriter plectrum.

Not that I want to limit it to earth,
Since it had outer space in also previously,
As well as grief, solemnity, and mirth,
And persons acting virtuously and deviously.
This follow-up of mine to *Ko* had birth
Fourteen years after, when I suffered feverishly
And feverishly wrote, to make an equal
Turmoil which came from me and caused a sequel—

Which intermittently I went on writing
With pleasure for two years. And, after that,
I stopped. I found some other things exciting
And left this epic I'd been working at.
And now the world has changed again, inviting
Me back to love, and Aqua Puncture's hat,
To Huddel's heart, to Papend's heat, and to
The mystery of Minnie Mouse's shoe;

To Alouette and him she would return to,
To Amos's statue, larger than a room—
This stanza is a help, a splendid churn to
Make oppositions one, to bring Khartoum,
Venice, and Oz into the self-same urn; to
Put silverfoil and rags on the same loom
Along with silks and wool and mud, to weave
A fabric to deceive and undeceive.

The problem is, Can I pick up my story
And carry it convincingly from where
I left it trailing an uncertain glory
Through the humming, bee-filled Venice air
And plunk it down again as in a dory
In my now elder words, perhaps more bare
Of connotation and my mind less leaping
Than when I saw you last when I was sleeping

And saw you blossom for me every night
Just like a girl and also like a field which
Was filled with flowers, daisies yellow white
And roses pink and white, a florist's yield which
Would make him think a horrid world all right—
So were you to me. Well, that loss is healed, which
Is not to say that I no longer love you,
Because I do. But I've stopped dreaming of you

In that particular way, which made me wild.
To wit, and to resume, I wonder if,
As I've grown further from the actual child
I used to be, I still can leap in skiff
And hope for the same wavy, undefiled
Trip through the aether like a hippogriff
I have had once, or several times, or always.
I think about these things sometimes in hallways

But when I reach the room and there's the door
And there's the typewriter with paper waiting,
I leap into my place, and, lo! before
I've had a second more for meditating,
I've filled up pages flitting to the floor
On which what seem like countless truths I'm stating;
Then darkness comes, or supper, and I stop it.
Next day the fear once more is Can I top it?

So, I suppose, on thinking the thing over,
Yes, I can take up where I left it lying
My poem which from the white cliffs of Dover
To Tuscany, where someone's hair is drying,
Goes quickly as a beam of light, that rover
Without compare, and with some honest trying
Continue my narration of the fallacy
We find by being born into this galaxy.

This galaxy in which—a fine word, *galaxy*,
Giving a sense of clean wide open spaces
In which there's nothing much to cause an allergy,
Which, bringing itch to throats and pink to faces,
Can get a person dropped from the anthology
Of health and beauty and ongoing graces;
And, as a word, it's a good test of diction;
Though it has overtones of science fiction,

Which, like all other special kinds of writing,
Is often dull save to aficionados,
As ravens, bats, and graveyards are exciting
To those who like to have their sex in grottos
But not to most, who fear the vampire's biting,
The sluggish worm, and the gravedigger Otto's
Hard shovel hitting them, or his bad jokes;
So psychedelic art's for one who smokes

Or eats the cactus bud or drops the acid,
And motorcycle jokes for one with bike.
The trouble with these genres is they're placid—
One knows right at the start what they'll be like.
Dog tales may please the owner of the basset
And barroom tales enthrall your Uncle Mike,
But those whose taste in things is more demanding
Prefer a story built on understanding

And not, like science fiction, seeing only
How new discoveries have changed conditions
So that you squeeze a module when you're lonely,
Or have your interests altered by physicians
Who are themselves machines, not flesh-and-bone-ly.
Such stuff is dull and can't compare to Titian's
High-flying saints or works of Proust or Byron,
Which are more complicated in their wiring

Just as I hope this work I'm writing may be,
In which it's true I found that *galaxy* suited
My meaning as a nursery fits a baby
Because its atmosphere's unconvoluted
And full of time and space and dark and day, be-
Cause it's grand and at the same time muted—
My characters, God bless them, have real lives in it
Like bees someplace with galaxies of hives in it,

Which there were not in Papend's Venice. Well,
I must confess that I don't quite feel ready
To leap back into things just yet and tell
How this and that were—I still feel unsteady:
Sometimes I ring with insights like a bell—
At others I feel close to Zacowitti!
I think I want to stall to tell you more
Of what I've felt, since on Hibernia's shore

I walked each day with Homer Brown and wrote
So many pages leading up to this one.
We'd see green fields so worthy of our note
That I at least was tempted to go kiss one.
But didn't, since I'm neither sheep nor goat,
But tried instead distilling all the bliss one
Feels in such happy times into my eight-line
Poetic sets with a late-sixties dateline—

And which will be resumed, but not this second.
I said I want to say things, and I do,
To catch myself and you up on the fecund,
Or fecund-seeming, life this long-lapsed Jew,
To whom the Talmud Torah had not beckoned
Imperiously since nineteen forty-two,
Lived since that time, but most to tell you of
That Irish time I wrote this, which I love

To think about, but I have never done so
At length at all because of life's fast pace
Which, starting off with waking, makes me run so
That I am short of breath and red of face
By evening, as if Tempus held a gun so
That Fugit could escape. Oh lovely lace
Of memory, that we can hold and contemplate—
How much of you mind's attic does accommodate!

There must be miles of you that are still folded
And stacked away in trunks I'll never get to!
Some people claim that some of theirs have molded—
I must confess mine I have not known yet to:
What I have Lear'd or Tristran-and-Isolde'd
Is with me still, each sit-down and each set-to,
For me to find the temporal space to climb to
And speculate about and find the rhyme to.

I want to do this now with those six weeks
I spent in Kinsale working on this epic
Which of things unattempted boldly speaks
In verse Orlandic, Don-Juanesque, and Beppic:
Of how Alaskan toucans got their beaks,
And why the waters of the vast Pacific
Are blue at dawn and pink by half past seven;
Of how things are on earth, and how in heaven—

A work perhaps I never can conclude.
It's my own fault—I like works to be endless,
So no detail seems ever to intrude
But to be part of something so tremendous,
Bright, clear, complete, and constantly renewed,
It totally obliterates addenda's
Intended use, to later compensate
For what was not known at the earlier date.

So, Memory, back! to those sweet times in Cork, which
Have not yet gotten my complete attention,
And, Muse! help me to find that tuning fork which
Makes anything it touches good to mention.
I'm starting up this work now in New York, which
Is as unlike Kinsale as hypertension
Is unlike pleasant calm and sunny weather—
By verse I hope to get them all together

And most specifically by verse concerning
The days I spent in Kinsale. Well, I've said that
At least two times already and am burning
To carry on this discourse with my head that
The world calls poetry and I call yearning—
If you don't mind, do please forget you read that:
It's far beneath my standards and I worry
You'll think it's me—it's not—I'm in a hurry

To catch my feelings while they pass me fleetingly
And so don't want to stop at every boner
Like scholars who er-umly and indeedingly
Lard everything so much you wish a stone or
A rowboat's oar would batter them obediently
Then magically fly back to its owner
Who thus would not be punished. I like catching
Pure chickens of discourse while they're still hatching

And so, unhushed, rush on. I had a bedroom
In that three-story house which the Browns lived in;
Each day I wrote my poem in the said room
While Betty Brown diced, sliced, and carved, and sieved in
The kitchen which was under it. The red room
Across the hall from mine, designed by Rifkin,
Homer and Betty dwelt in, and the other
Room on that floor was Katherine's, whom her mother

Would sing to sleep two times a day or once,
Depending if she was in a napping period;
When she was, there was one nap after lunch
Or sometimes none, at which time cries were myriad
And I would set my elbow with a crunch
Upon the desk and, like a man much wearièd
By journey long across a perilous waste,
Put head in hand and groan as one disgraced

By having lost all natural zest for living,
All inspiration, talent, luck, and skill.
I've always thought I should be more forgiving
And not be seized by the desire to kill
When someone interrupts me at my knitting
Of words together, but I'm that way still.
I've not, however, murdered anyone,
I swear, as I am Stuart and Lillian's son.

How moved I am to write their names, how curious
They sound to me, as Kenneth does, my own one,
Which, though I'm no more Scots than Madame Curie is,
I like for the plain clear Highlandsy tone one
(Or I) can hear in it. Some names sound spurious,
Like "Impsie," or Sir Lalla Rookh Ben Lomond.
Some are invented; some we choose by fantasy;
Some hoping to inherit; some, romantically—

If, for example, Dad once loved a lassie
Named Billy Jo, he might call baby Billy,
If baby is a boy, or if the chassis
Of that small creature shows that it is silly
To think she's the same sex as Raymond Massey
And may one day play Lincoln, perhaps Tillie
Might satisfy his crazed nostalgic need
To see his old flame at his wife's breast feed.

In any case, names are a sort of token
Which parents give a child when it sets out
Into life's subway system, which is broken
And filled with people eating sauerkraut;
We pass the turnstile when our name is spoken
But it's the train that hurries us about,
I.e. our brain, brawn, energy, and genius,
Whether we're named Kaluka or Frobenius.

So names begin us, but—On with my story!
If I have interrupted interruptions
Of interrupted interruptions, glory
Will never be my lot, but foul corruptions;
For that which feeds upon itself grows gory—
But there, again, enough! All my productions
Are subject to this peril; let's go on.
Already in the east I see the dawn

Growing more quickly than the flush of red
Upon the back of Lisa who has lain
Four hours naked in the sand instead
Of going to the store at Fifth and Main
To buy some pinking scissors as she said
That she was going to, wherefore her pain;
And out of the vague silence of the night
Come clippery sounds of birds, not yet in flight.

So did the mornings greet me in Kinsale,
Often, when I would read all night, or, oftener,
When I would have some nightmare by the tail
Which crushed the woof of sleep like fabric softener
And brought me naked to the shade, where pale
Aurora seemed, as Joyce said, to be "doffin' 'er
Glarious gowrments to receive the Sun"—
Those garbs were pink and red. O Day begun,

How energizing so to contemplate you
Before the full awareness of the twenty-
Four hours we have to know you makes us hate you,
Sometimes; sometimes one minute of you's plenty
And makes one wish to ante- or post-date you
Just so you go away—but in the denty
Sweet early scuds of dawning, how delicious
You, Day, can be! so that, sometimes, ambitious

Poets have hailed you at your birth with names
Like Monday, Tuesday, Thursday, Friday, Sunday,
Saturday, Wednesday, Pottsday, Day of Flames,
Day of Decision, Pet and Family Fun Day,
All Fools Day, Hallowe'en, Christmas, Henry James
Commemorative Reading Day, Clean Gun Day,
Happy Hog Day, and so on, as if, by calling
You names, one might prevision your befalling

Or something of that kind. Well, at the window
Sometimes I'd stay a while and sometimes hurry
Back into bed whose sheets like very thin dough
Were slightly rough for sleeping (made by Murray)
And doze again, then later would begin to
Get dressed for breakfast, which, in a great flurry
Of soda bread, we three would eat together
With Katherine Brown, in the cold Irish weather.

Then after that quite often I would run
Along a kind of sidewalk that ran upwards
From where the house was, up to where the sun
Would have been closer if in the cloudy cupboards
It did not hang away till day was done.
Then homeward, past proud dames in Mother Hubbards
And former Irish exiles who'd found out
That Budweiser was nothing to the stout

Served at "The Spaniard" on Saint Bernard's Hill.
Sometimes "Good marnin" would emerge from these
I passed, and sometimes not, for they were still
And I was running, it was not with ease
We could converse. My lungs with breath would fill,
My heart with beats, and then my mind would seize
Sometimes a phrase or line that made me race to
Get back in time so I could find a place to

Put it into my poem in time to carry
With it all its inspired associations.
One's words, though, once excited, mate and marry
Incessantly, incestuously, like patients
Gone mad with love, so even sometimes the very
Words I would lose enroute spawned duplications
Stretching as far as sight. Back at my desk
I'd sit then, breathless and Chirrurgeresque

With lacy inspirations and complexities
Made up of breath and heartbeats and confusions,
As one may have of fish as to what sex it is,
As to which of my *trouvailles* were delusions
And which could guide my poem as sheep executives
Ideally guide their flocks, toward such effusions
Of epic lyric life that I would find
The sole true story of man's secret mind.

A large ambition! Strange that words suggest to us
That we can do such things. And strange the feeling
That we have done it sometimes; strange that Aeschylus
Probably felt the same beneath the ceiling
Of the Greek room he wrote in for the festivals
Of le Théâtre Grec. And it is healing
The thought that one is capable in some way
Of being in control on this huge Stunway

Of our existence. Anyway, I'd sit
Un-Aeschylean, certainly, at that
Table I used for desk, and stretch my wit
In such way as I could. There was a flat
Quality to my living there that fit
The kind of thing that I was working at;
Friendly but not involved with anyone
Not lonely, but, whenever I wished, alone.

And there were, doubtless, certain real connections
Of other kinds between my life and work
About the Early Girls with belle complexions
And Papend more licentious than a Turk,
And Huddel who can fly in all directions
And Mugg McDrew who now in Death did lurk—
Some ways in which cool Kinsale did concur
With Aqua, but I don't know what they were.

Well, maybe, this: a kind of a suspension
Of everything except my poem, which filled
The spaces action left with pure invention
Of characters beaked, snouted, nosed, and billed.
Then, too, there was that sweet unnerving tension
Travel creates, the worst parts of it stilled
By being with my friends. And then there was
The foghorn, so like Inspiration's buzz.

Enough! My story's sun should now come out, when
I'm feeling I am fit to make it good—
How happy, though, I've been to write about then,
That time I walked on Kinsale's sea-soaked wood
With Betty and Homer Brown and had no doubt then
That all would be completed, as it should
Have been. How glad to think again of walks
I took with Homer and, at night, the talks

With Homer and with Betty, while we heard
Sitting in the garden chairs above the house
Halfway to where "The Spaniard's" barmaids spurred
The local gentry nightly to carouse
With dark black Guinness—in the garden burred
With tiny burrs no bigger than a louse,
The seabirds calling—really did they call?
Or was there nothing in that sound at all

But bird phonetics, sea phonetics, what?
And if someone had come to me to say,
Wishing, perhaps, to put me on the spot,
"Just what's the content of your work today?"
I could say, "Not abstractions, though it's not,
Either, the sounds of birds on Kinsale Bay,
But human sounds, make of them what you want to;
Saying unto others as I've been said unto—

Trying to put into a usable range
A vast amount of matter, form, and tone
(Which is what human noises are) to change
What seems disparate into what alone
Can make us happy: re-possession. Strange!
That we should be so different from a stone!
But since we are, I'll go on writing this way.
For other modes, see Dryden, Pope, and Disney;

See Wordsworth in this rustical abode;
(Not Shelley though for he resembles me
In twitching off his story like a toad
So he can dream of what it is to be
A crag of icy flame or a lone road
Amid the Apennines, or a blue sea
Of expectation and despair) see Cowper
A very quiet but consistent trouper

Of Things That Really Happen, in the Order
In which they do. For all of these and most
Of those who wrote before the Abstract Border
Of this odd twentieth century was crossed
A Structure had to be of stone and mortar
Or it could not exist. Let's drink a toast
To Rimbaud and Apolinaire and laughter,
And all who, learning from them, have come after

To practice this new art. The purpose of it?
I think I have already said, but one
Keeps asking. It is to help people love it,
Their world, I mean, which has such means to stun,
Confuse, and kick. But one can be above it
And in it all at once, it can be done
If poets do what I believe they're meant to,
I.e. the whole of what they feel give vent to."

"Farewell!" With this digression from digressing
I'll go back to my story. Though not all
Of what went on in Kinsale—it's depressing
To think what's gone from summer by the fall—
Is talked about, I've gotten back the pressing
Desire I had, as lofty as a wall
And twice as strong, to write. So let this vanish
Into the mountain air above the Spanish

Part of the Pyrenees and, even higher,
Where we left Aqua Puncture and her lover
In flight from death and strengthened by desire
Among the curious clouds, where they discover
Sky nutriment of all kinds they require,
At which they have looked wildly at each other
Hoping a hopeless hope, that they might stay
There in that soft perpetual blue-white day.

"*Légumes des cieux!*" breathed Aqua. "Well, but still
We've found no place that we can sit or stand."
Huddel said, "Over there, this little hill
Of cloud. Try! Yes! It's solid, love, as sand
Firmed by the grand Atlantic's azure spill!"
So they two sat down on it. With her hand
Aqua touched his. "If we could find more solid
Cloud, might we . . . ?" Her with his hands he collared

And kissed her hard: her mouth, her lips, her eyes.
"We can! We will!" He walked and looked around.
He found one mile-long stretch, a grand surprise,
Which seemed to be as solid as the ground.
"That's it! Wait here! I'll go get some supplies
From earth—" but, thinking, then: "They can be found,
Perhaps, right here." He smiled. "We may not need
So very much," he said. Aqua agreed.

This was a good decision, since beneath them
(Just fifteen feet beneath) there was a pack
Of sky piranhas in a mood to eat them,
If they had seen them, on a watery track
That went from Rome to somewhere east of Eden—
Some colored green and blue, some white and black.
The leading one, Piranha Ninety-Six,
Had taught her fellow-fish some aero-tricks

Which made them capable of "swimmo-flying,"
A mode of locomotion known in Dallas
On the Aereal Lakes, built by a dying
Billionaire to fête his girlfriend Alice
On one of her young birthdays. She, untying
The laces of her stays, cried, "Oh, a palace
Of airy pools!" Then in each other's arms
These two were happy, till he left her charms,

That very year, for death. His girl went on
To be the world's great star in this aquatic,
Celestial sport. How many a summer dawn
Saw her fair form amidst it, she the product
Of human kind, yet equal to the swan
In water, dove in air. An old despotic
Aquarium man had taught his prize piranha
The trick, as well. Now, pale as a Madonna

Of Piero's, Aqua saw them and was shaken—
"H-Huddel, l-l-look—" With her right hand
She pointed to the fish, which now had taken
A downward turn, and soon their deadly band
Had swimmo-flown away and left forsaken
Them, glad to be. And now they walked and planned
A new existence in the clouds till when
Something might draw them to the earth again.

It's difficult to stay away forever
From something we have lived with all our lives,
Or most of them. All find it hard to sever
Relations with their husbands or their wives.
So with our native planet. And what bever-
Age ever shall, with sharpness as of knives,
Give us that high, like Legions back in Rome again,
When we return to earth, of being home again?

Now, though, they feel contented to remain
In their sky nest forever. For, aside from
Their love, what had life offered them but pain?
Oh pleasant place. Far off from there now glide from
Blue to blue-white the sky-piranha chain
Of Ninety-Six, which anyone would hide from
Who knew the eating habits of these predators,
Sea-homnivores of sky. Meanwhile the editors

Of papers everywhere observed the progress
Of the Great Hellas Race, now much diminished
By Mickey's absence, which encouraged codgers
Who'd bet on him before to say, He's finished!
The Rats will win, as surely as Buck Rogers
Will conquer Killer Kane. As if a tin dish'd
Move sideways from a dog, while they were speaking
Tobacco moved across their jaws. And, squeaking,

Terence and Alma Rat enjoy the full
Fanfare of earthly stardom. They are left,
They only, left! as in the ring the bull
When matador is missing, it bereft
Of everything but Toro in the cool
Of Spanish afternoon! He felt so deft,
Terence, at his red steering wheel, and stormed
Up and down roads which Grecian hillsides formed.

"Oh, Alma dear, this is the only life
That's fit for such a couple, whose ambition
Is to be more than merely rat and wife
But to exceed in glorious condition
The sun itself, which glistens like a knife
Upon us rats in summer! The ignition
Seems to be out of order—help! What's happened?"
The car stopped. He looked ghastly, as if rat-penned.

"Terence, what's wrong?" cried Alma. She looked over
And saw a deadly serpent on the seat
Just beside Terence. "I am Herman Clover,"
The serpent said, "Come, listen to me, Sweet."
Then made a gesture to draw near which drove her
To the Toyota door on quick rat feet.
"What—why—who—ah!" she cried. He coolly said
"Don't worry about your rat. He isn't dead.

I gave him just a little bit of venom,
Enough to stop his driving. He'll be fine.
He will awake with a slight taste of cinnam-
On in his mouth, and you, dear, will be mine!"
He seized her in his coils, which caused a cinem-
Athèque in Athens to explode and nine
Persons to suffer in Constantinople
From heart disease. The snake produced an opal

From his long mouth, which, offering to the rodent
He seemed to love so much, at least to long for
And want to touch, which is an urge prepotent
In all, but snakes especially are strong for
Tactile sensations of their whole belowment,
Which they are willing even to do wrong for,
At least by human lights, he sighed, "I love you.
This whole long season I've been thinking of you."

"No! No!" He squeezed her. "I'm in love with Terence!"
She saw him slumped against the steering wheel
Like someone who is running interference
Caught in a stop-shot. The automobile
Was not much longer graced by her appearance—
The snake had tugged her out. Great waves of steel
Atop a concrete ocean—"It's terrific,"
Said Pemmistrek. Ann said, "Be more specific.

There're parts of modern art which are so difficult
For me and others of us Early Girls.
We usually keep silent, fearing ridicule,
But I think I can ask you why these swirls
Of metal water are at all aesthetical?"
Our scene has changed, it's evident, to curls
Of human heads, away from leap- and crawl-ers—
To whom we shall return. Be such the solace

Of all who wish to know what happened next
To frightened Alma and the terrible worm
Who seemed to be so interspecies-sexed
With his great, diamond-studded epiderm,
Who's gazing at her, hoping she'll be hexed
And he can bring his passion to its term
With this small animal, whose doubts we know of.
So Pemmistrek, with one toe from the toe of

One sock protruding—it was glorious spring
Which topped all Stockholm with its towering green
And he had taken his shoes off, like a thing
That anyone would do, but as we've seen
He's childlike, since amnesiac, and a king
Would give his crown I think to have a bean
So full of sweet oblivion and pleasure
As his was, and would add his queen and treasure—

Stood looking at the outdoor show of art
Of modern times and liking it, and Ann was
Puzzling about it, when they heard the start
Of a huge car, of which it seemed the plan was
To run them down. My God! it must be smart
To find a way to be as the first man was,
Adam, I mean, exempt from, in the soft spring,
Attack from others, either strange or offspring!

But not since then, I think, has any managed
To have complete protection. Even Adam
Was by his earthly consort disadvantaged
When she brought him an apple. Thank you, Madam.
Oh well, all right! Then boom! Boom, doom, and damaged,
We have not yet recovered from that datum
(If it is true, which cannot be gone into)
For, ground beneath the wheels of a great Pinto

Grey Stockholm gravel flies in Pemmistrek's face,
And he grabs Ann in one arm and ducks under
The huge car's under part which leaves them place
To go on living while a noise like thunder
Goes past above their heads. God, for a mace!
Cried Pemmistrek, with which to rend asunder
This goddamned car which wants to run us down!
The car sped past them, though, deep into town.

Inside this vehicle was a musician
Named Fine McStrings, a Protestant and Scottish
Who falsely had attained the high position
Of Royal Rabbi, whose main job was Kaddish,
And, needing practice for a new rendition
Of this prayer for the dead—abstractly moddish
As other versions weren't—was multiplying
As best he could, the number of the dying,

Hoping to thus get practice in his service
Before some Royal Family member perished.
Performing before others made him nervous,
And any public things he did he cherished
He had to do until he felt impervious
To his embarrassment. Now with a glare Ist-
Anbul comes into focus, and the hospital
Where a young woman lies, fair as a rose petal—

Not by McStrings run down, but one of those who
Got heart disease when Herman Clover coiled
Himself round Alma. Lucky are the clothes who,
Or which, touch her sweet body, lucky boiled
Eggs that her tongue delects, and lucky No-Shu,
Her Chinese lover, until now unfoiled
By rival—man or malady—now saddened
Up to the point of being completely maddened.

This girl is an important nuclear physicist
And translator of Proust into Icelandic
Named Norma Clune. I wish that she would visit us,
If she gets well, this side of the Atlantic,
For everywhere she goes the nation's business
Improves, and all its men become romantic.
No one's been able to explain this power—
But now she's threatened by her final hour . . .

Which great physicians, flying in from Stockholm,
Nome, and Peru, are striving to prevent.
Her crazy No-Shu wants to run and sock them
Or bash them with a torn-loose tenement.
That man who touches Norma is unwelcome
As far as he's concerned. He had been bent
By horrible experiences when he
Was five years old that caused this jealousy.

His father and his mother had a dog
Named Uncle Patsy, Ki-Wa in Chinese,
Which bumblebees had trapped under a log.
No-Shu, just five, ran out and chased the bees
But then got lost, while going home, in fog
And had a vision of his mother's knees
With someone's hand upon them. Since that time
He had devoted half his life to crime.

He went round killing people in strange ways
Whom he suspected of unfaithful loving.
Be careful! or you, too, one of these days,
May be the victim of a fatal shoving
And be fished up from one of various bays,
Or ground in little bits to be the stuffing
Of the large Christmas turkey that No-Shu
Sends each December to the O.N.U.,

Now that Mao's China's been admitted to it.
Norma, who loves him even though he's crazy,
Had made him go each week to Dr. Bluet,
The psychiatric heir of Piranesi,
Who saw man's mind as a huge, complex cruet
In which he was imprisoned, like a daisy.
He'd worked with No-Shu now for eighteen months,
Who in that period had killed only once.

But now he rages through the hospital's halls
Screaming in horror at his sweetheart's illness.
Doctors propose removing No-Shu's balls
If he does not cooperate more with stillness.
They throw him out. He pounds upon the walls
And plans revenge; and Head Nurse Olga Hilness
Sees Doctor Adam Shrude and feels her heart skip
One tiny beat, and, moored outside, an art ship

Rocks on the Bosporus, filled with many treasures,
Among which a large black and white of Mickey
And Minnie Mouse, a painting, with the pleasures
Great works of art can give, and give them quickly
By power of paint and shape and line. It measures
Six hundred square hectares, which makes it tricky
To get it on the boat and, once aboard it,
To find an angle from which to regard it.

This giant portrait, made by the joint efforts
Of fifty painters in the U.S.A.,
England, and Greece, was to protest the severance
Of Mickey from real life. The painters, they
Felt that a work so huge construed in reference
To this event might touch him where he lay.
By some strange chance it does. In comics sleep
On Sunday papers, he begins to squeak.

This painting's strong effect upon the real
Is not unique, although unusual:
A sculpture of a Minnesota Seal
Once caused the other team to lose the ball;
Motshubi's *Young Girl with Banana Peel*
Caused fifty-five young men to leap, or fall,
From Yomo Bridge; and Titian's *Presentation*
Caused Tintoretto's, and its estimation.

Another case, well-known as far as Knossos,
Is how Pissarro, Sisley, and Monet,
By certain kinds of brush and color process,
Made different-colored dots appear all day
On air, clouds, stones, walls, ponds, Parisian *places*,
Cathedrals, sailboats, woods, and stacks of hay.
Mickey, through similar process, leaps to life
And says good morning to his waking wife:

"Minnie! I've had a vision—and a hope!
Of what I ought to do. If I could win
After all, win the race, and somehow grope
My way to Sounion mid discordant din
Of gear and crankshaft up the final slope,
Then to the attending world admit my sin
And weep in penance for it, might not that
Be what would be the best? Watch out! a cat!"

Cried Mickey, and, until the tom had passed,
He did not say a word. Meanwhile the island
Of Crete had grown a little bit more vast
Due to the shellfish, which, as always, silent
As to what their intentions were, had massed
Against its very shore, so that a pilot
Flying above it thought it was Australia.
And Terence Rat picked a light pink azalea

For Alma in his dream. And Mickey uttered
His first sound in a while. "I think it's safe.
Now I must try to rise from here," he muttered,
And struggled. "I'll come with you!" She was brave
And loved her mouse when every candle guttered
Of hope for peace and joy. They felt a wave
Of useful force communicated by
The work of art, and rose into the sky,

Leaving the papers torn where they'd been slumbering
Day after day in plain and color comics.
Now over Thessaly they fly, encumbering
The April air, blown higher than the summits
Of Mount Olympus, known to us as numbering
Amongst its gods Athena quick of comments,
Zeus filled with enterprise, and Aphrodite
Most beautiful of girls, whom, in her nightie,

Each girl each night may look like to her love.
Here in these vaults of heaven it was spring
Eternal, and yet changing, like a glove
Or a goodbye, white stairways opening,
And walks that one could not grow tired of.
It was quite obviously the very thing
A human would desire—it was created
By men, in fact, it's said, who abdicated

It to the gods. Now to its summits glided
Mickey and Minnie, the mysterious energy
The artwork gave them having much subsided.
Apollo sees their landing as a prodigy
Of some Divine Good Luck, and they're invited
To stay forever, Mickey to be God of the
Repentant Heart, and Minnie of Fidelity.
Hard to resist is the superior melody

Of these Olympian voices, and the mouse pair,
At last, resist it not. The race abandoned
By them remains, but they can do good elsewhere
By being little gods. And if their fandom
(The artists, chiefly, and those in the house where
There are gross effigies of them in sand and
Clay and cement, in Houston) is not satisfied,
Well, others are. In Athens, where the fat is fried

All day upon the gridiron, Postulakis,
The Cretan cook, whose specialty is octopus,
Known round the whole Aegean, throws a cactus
Into his stew and cries, "Yes, there are lots of us
Who love those mice, and even, yes, the fact is,
Revere them, as if gods, which is half-cocked of us
You may suppose, but now, you see, it's authorized!"
He left the cactus in till it was cauterized

Then plucked it out and poured in what seemed tons
Of olive oil and gristle. And Jose
Jorge Romero, of Iberia's sons
The greatest dancer down Flamenco way,
Cried, "These ees what ees really good, for once,
Zat zees two mice be gods!" And bronzed Earl Grey
Looked up from his tea laboratory stirrings
With appreciative whimperings and purrings—

For Earl Grey was a cat, as few men knew.
It had been hidden from his wife, who rarely
Shared Earl Grey's bed. Then would he, dressed in blue,
Propel a human plastic doll he barely
Could manage to keep moving, to her, who
Would fold it in her arms and love it yarely.
Earl Grey, inside the doll, would meditate
On what had caused him such a curious fate.

Next day, the doll undone, once more he was
Tea Lord of All, and, hearing of the mice,
Even he, a cat and avid for their fuzz,
Expressed his joy for them. I've said that twice,
And now away to Stockholm, where the buzz
Of the King's voice turns someone cold as ice.
King Sven has learned of his false rabbi's murders
And has condemned him to be hung from girders

To be devoured by Swedish ants. "Not that!"
McStrings exclaims, but oh, his fate is sealed.
Next day his skeleton, devoid of fat,
Swings from the Rathaus flagpole, like a shield
Some thoughtless soldier hung there. With no hat
Upon his head, or hers, like one unreeled
From a great spool of gladness, Pemmistrek
With Ann goes by, and does not see that wreck.

Where they will go when they have loved their full
In icy Stockholm, causing curious copies
Of cities to spring up, an Istanbul
With dark guitars, a Rome with yellow poppies
Instead of red, a Bogota *azul*
As summer ocean wherein lies the porpoise,
We soon shall see, but now I'd like to go
To Papend—but cannot quite yet although

I wished it, for Alouette just now arrives
In Stockholm's airport, and this fact demands
Attention. To the cabby as he drives
Her into town she's talking with her hands
Because she knows no Swedish. Then she dives
Out of the taxi, pays her fare, and lands
Inside the swell hotel to which she's driven,
Which caters specially to famous women—

The Stockholmbusgeflossen. Norma Clune
Once rested here, between her Proust translations
And Olla, the first woman on the moon,
And Dr. Anne McFeedbach and the patients
Who traveled with her. This hotel at noon
Gave a great lunch, with generous libations,
And Alouette, now, arrived at the meridian,
Sits down to eat among the grey obsidian

Of the Geflossen's architecture. She thinks
Of Pemmistrek and of the Munster Mooson,
Her own hotel in Asia, as she drinks
A glass of aquavit, which tends to loosen
One's hold upon reality. She sinks
Into a deep, drugged sleep, which is quite gruesome
As far as her projected project goes.
For Pemmistrek is leaving Stockholm! Rose,

An Early Girl whose lover is a captain
In the Stockholm police force, finds him murdered—
His nose and ears cut off and his skull fractured,
What deep hostility was thus asserted
Or disapproval of how he'd been acting.
She did not know, but feared, for she had heard it
Had been because of her, because Yorg Berls
Now knew the secret of the Early Girls.

Berls was a young ecologist. Once knowing
That every time an Early Girl made love
A city came to be, his red blood flowing
Too quickly to his brain made him one of
Those persons who to doctors should be going
To be calmed down with pills. A dark red glove
Of craziness obscured his mind. He wildly
Set out to kill all those who loved so mildly,

So sweetly, and so well these Early Ladies
Who weren't really causing any harm—
The cities they created were like Maybes
From someone who is feeling nice and warm
And whom a later sequence shows with babies
Or smiling through the rafters of a barn—
I.e. they didn't last long. Berls, however,
Killed ignorantly in the soft Stockholm weather.

So that this murder would be Berls's last
It seemed most wise to leave. Crazed Berls himself
Was later killed by No-Shu—but that ghast-
Ly tale must wait for later. Now the shelf
Of the Nord-Sud Express's bathroom passed
The shelf of Igborg Mountain, where the Elf
Igborgo lived, according to the fable.
The train had to be pulled on a big cable,

And in it, eating soup, sat Pemmistrek
And Early Ann and Early Rose, and other
Nearby compartments' windows showed the neck
And face and shoulders of the Captain's brother,
And those of other Early Girls and, check
To see if all of them are there, their lovers.
Alouette, elsewhere, asleep, dreams she's a photon,
Ten billion times too small to leave a note on

Somebody's door to say that you'd come by
To say hello, though you have other reasons,
Just as the cloudblooms have some in the sky
To make it seem like spring at other seasons,
And as the wind to make the pollen fly—
And in this curious dream knew the obeisance
That Matter has to Energy! She woke,
And at her ear a terrible voice spoke:

"You have been given information which
A mortal may not have. Prepare to die.
For you cannot continue in this ditch
Of ordinary living. Now the sky
Invites you to its realms, where there's no hitch.
You will be happy there!" She: "Oh will I?
I don't believe it. Please! I am attached
To what is here, and I would not be snatched

Away from it!" Now the hotel began
To bustle with the sounds of early dinners,
For Alouette's sleep had, like a caravan,
Stretched from high noon to that hour which the Finnish
Call "*Eep van artom*," time to get a man
Or woman to be with, and while a thinnish
Old waiter turns up glasses, Sol is soldering
The last blue bolts of day, and mouths are watering

For dinner and, once more, for aquavit,
Which Swedish tipplers know as "The Superb."
A man sees Alouette get up from her seat
And walks across to her. "My name is Herb
McFuel. I saw you turn white as a sheet
Of paper which ten sticks of chalk disturb
And wondered if I could be of assistance."
Alouette said, "You'd better keep your distance,

For I'm about to die and be transported
To heavenly realms, and you might be dragged with me
If you're too close." His answer's not recorded
For just that instant a huge jug of whiskey
Was drunk in Texas and a plane was boarded
By someone whom the reader knows from Disney,
Pluto the Pup, who has been working there,
Since leaving Greece, for Papend. Through the air

He flies to Second Venice, where he's handed
An envelope, inside which is a letter
To Aqua Puncture from that man so candid
About desire that none was ever better.
"Oh find her if you can!" And now he's landed,
Pluto, where never terrier, toy, or setter
Had put down paws before—on solid clouds.
"Good heavens!" Huddel cried, "Does this mean crowds

Of people on the Earth know where we are?
Tell us, Sir, how you found us." Pluto smiled,
Or looked that certain way which on our star
We say is a dog smiling. It was mild
And sun-warmed breezy weather. In his car
Apollo rolled about the airs, beguiled,
Himself, at so much beauty. Pluto said,
"I just got this idea in my head

That since Commander Papend could not find you,
With all his messengers, in any country
On earth, that you, perhaps, had put behind you
The earth as someplace alien and bumpy,
Too full of those who menaced and maligned you,
And left it altogether for such sundry
New places as might be—rouge sunrise passes,
Air halls, snowflake pavilions, white cloud masses.

I got myself a little plane and tried
A thousand places till I came to this one.
So no one knows of you." "But," Huddel sighed,
"Who's Papend, who has sent you on this mission?"
"It is all in the letter." He ran wide
Around his plane and fetched it, an efficient
And mostly clever dog, whose sexual preference
Has earlier been the subject of a reference.

"Aqua's out gathering crocodiles," said Huddel—
"What?" Pluto cried—"We'll wait a while till she
Returns, and then she'll read it." "I'm not subtle
Enough to know what 'crocodiles' might be,"
Said Pluto. "Are there real ones?" A befuddle-
D expression clouds his eyes. "No mystery!"
Laughs Huddel. "They're a certain kind of lettuce
Which Aqua likes and sometimes goes to get us.

It's very good in sky *salade*." "The name, though,"
The dog persists, "how did it get its name?"
Huddel began to say; then Aqua came, though,
And they abandoned their linguistic game
On seeing her appearing, like a rainbow.
"Hello!" she said to Pluto, and a flame
Danced in her eye. "What's this? A billet-doux?"
Then evening marched across, in darkened blue.

Aqua sits down and reads. Rereads. And she
At last has read the letter Papend sent,
By every method everywhere that he
Could think of, to his sister, whom he meant
To know, at last, and be with. On one knee,
Which like the other's loveliest when bent,
She rests the hand in which the letter flutters
In the night breeze, at which she sometimes shudders

And sometimes not. "Oh best of things and worst!
A brother, a connection with the past
And with the life I did not have at first
And with the world I wandered from at last
To live in love when living was accursed!
O double judgment on my judging passed!"
She sighed, "I feel I must go see my brother."
He said, "Well, you do not have any other—

We ought to go." She cried, relieved. Dog barked.
"Come to my town of Venice for a visit,"
The letter said with which the dog embarked.
"Yes, we can try," said Huddel. "Oh don't miss it!"
The dog said, then round where the plane was parked
He ran awhile, and with this run's assistance
Had a huge appetite, which was diminished
By crocodile *salade* (it tastes like spinach

But it is slightly better, when uncooked)
A short while later, and some sky-blue cheeses.
New feelings now in Aqua were unhooked
And left her unprotected in the breezes
Of early night, at which she sat and looked
Like one whom something pleases and displeases
At the same time. And then she gave up trying
And let herself be overcome by crying.

O brotherhood and sisterhood, how sweet
How very sweet you are, or sweet you can be!
To have small playmates with the same size feet
And hands and head and tastes for the same candy!
To sit together all in the same seat
And be all muddy, slimy, wet, or sandy—
Not having any such in early years
Was what made Aqua now dissolve in tears.

While she sits crying, a tremendous goat
Is walking through that part of Thessaly
In which the rat-pair's car like a docked boat
Is stalled for lack of any energy,
Propulsive, to propel it. We should note
That this is not a goat, in truth, we see
But three Thessalian monks out doing penance
For having wished to visit Second Venice.

Father Propriades, discovering this
In dark and rocky mountain-top confession,
Had bade the lustful holy men to kiss
The cross and, in a sort of a procession,
Inside a goat's hide which gave emphasis
To just what sort of sin caused this digression
From ordinary monkish life atop
Mount Athos, where the prayers never stop

And where no female creature is permitted—
The opposite of Venice! even Ann
The Ant and Fay the Firefly are excluded,
And viruses themselves must be a man
In order to come in, or else are booted
Like Emperor Hirohito of Japan
Out, he by free elections, virus by
This monkish force that lives quite near the sky,

To walk the roads of Thessaly until
They could prevent an act of lawless lust.
Now, when this goat of men came down the hill
And saw poor Alma pinioned to the dust
It started leaping. Herman gave a shrill,
High cry of snake despair and left in trust
(And haste) his precious rat lass to the churchmen
Who quickly broke the goatskin dry as parchment

And ran to her defense. She needed none,
But only, now, reviving. For she'd fainted.
They gave her smelling salts, a special one
That Tintoretto sniffed each time he painted
Which made his hand go swiftly as a gun
In his delineations of the sainted.
And she revives. They bless her. To the car
She races. And shakes Terence. "Is it far?"

The poor chap asks her. "Darling you've been sleeping!
We've had an awful time! But those good fellows"—
She waved to where the monks were gladly speaking
To one another of the daylight's yellows
And of the azure air, then did a Greek thing
Of leaping through the air while making bellows
Of pleasure and relief that they had expi-
Ated their bad wishes to be sexy

And now were free to be themselves once more,
Not walk in a dried goatskin—"Those good persons
Came to my rescue. Now let's go! Before
That evil snake returns with his excursions
Against my loyalty!" She locked her door,
And Terence gave himself to the exertions
Of starting up the car, but was unable
To make it run. So there upon the table

Of Western Greece's geological furniture
They stay, till they are rescued by a Sodomite
Named Arpel D. McShanes, the famous Senator
From Arkansas who with a keg of dynamite
Blew up Three Rivers Stadium when the manager
Refused to give him tickets, which epitomized
His whole career. He was a violent citizen
In private life and public most unreticent.

He found the rodent pair a short time later
And gave them food and water and a lift
To Thebes, where they could buy a carburetor.
In fact, he gave one to them as a gift,
And wished them luck, then, Senatorial satyr,
Cruised factory workers getting off the shift
At OEDI-PANS, the kitchen factory Thebans
Kept busier than the mind of Wallace Stevens.

This plant had given the first hope of prosperity
To Thebes since ancient times. Its product, kitchenware,
Was made with the same beautiful form and clarity
As Classical Greek jars had been, enriching where
One was accustomed, if not to vulgarity,
At least to plainness. Aristotle Itching Bear,
A Greek American Indian got the idea
One day in boyhood from his Mother, Clea,

A striking woman ninety-five years old
At present, but at that time twenty-nine—
Sitting cross-legged in the tent, she told
Her pale papoose of Greece's sad decline.
Later, the little boy discovered gold
While playing catch beneath a clinging vine.
Investing it, and saving, he was zealous,
And finally he could make this gift to Hellas:

A mighty factory in which ancient crafts
Were brilliantly and gladly resurrected—
The men who worked there all were taught by staffs
Of the best artists that could be collected.
Outside this plant, McShanes the solon laughs
With somebody with whom he has connected.
They go off arm in arm, his bright green overcoat
Heaving with cheer, as in a storm the Dover boat.

Alma and Terence, then, with the Toyota
In running order, start it up and plunge
Into the Classical landscape, where no motor
Was heard in ancient days, till, like a sponge
Of green in deep green water, the iota
Of what they are has vanished. "I've a hunch,"
Said Papend, "from some curious sounds I've heard,
Which on the Grand Canal has twice occurred,

That some bizarre, unknown event is brewing
In my dear city. What, though, is its nature?"
He stands there in the soft May light, reviewing
A plan to change his city's architecture
By tinting all the matzoh walls with blueing.
"I think I won't," he said. "For in the future
The dye might eat the matzoh meal away
And giant bees of us make holiday."

He turned, in thought. Then a gigantic rattle
Was heard in Second Venice. Papend rushed
From one place to the next, as if in battle,
To find its source so that it could be hushed
But he found nothing, neither in the sattel-
Ite isles of the Lagoon, nor in the slushed
Sideways with aqua alta. Could it be
An earthquake? an uprising of the sea?

It was in fact that haughty Indian lord,
Son of the Inca, who, preserved in stone,
For several hundred years, did now afford
The day the pleasure of his Royal groan
As he shot up to freedom. Those on board
The vaporetto saw him wildly thrown
Above the Gritti Palace and be caught
Upon the Campanile's upmost spot.

He climbed down to the balcony which goes
Around it and gazed out at the strange city
And closed his eyes and almost kept them closed,
But no—he had escaped from Zacowitti,
He was alive—he touched his cheek, his nose,
Then looked again, then looked back at the Gritti,
Then wept a little. He felt very strange.
Here is the story, in English, of his change

Which he told Papend later. Papend managed
To understand it, mostly. It was curious—
And moving. This young king, half-dead and bandaged,
In secret to disguise him from the furious
And brutal vengeful Spaniards had been sandwiched
Between two slabs of granite, the notorious
Ninety-five edged ones which touristic drinkers
Swear is the greatest thing about the Incas.

Here wedged, he'd lasted, till some odd explosions
Of late (those Papend heard while round about
The Grand Canal on generous excursions)
Had started knocking him so much about
That he regained his senses. Then the Russians
Set off a bomb they told no one about
And he was thrown into the air. "But what
Is all of this?" he cried. So Papend got

A chance to tell him everything, which this
Young man was dazed by. "You know, it's uncanny,
But in the old place here I'd come to kiss
The prettiest girls—you've never seen so many!
Here on this very mountain top, my bliss
Was raised to such a height that the Great Bunny
Himself could know no more." He spoke of terraces,
Then, too, and made a number of comparisons

Of Macchu Picchu then and Venice now.
"We had no water here except for rain.
The land had trees, with blossoms on the bough.
We thought the earth was hung on a great chain
Which tied around the neck of a huge cow,
Whose name, 'Athpatala,' means 'super brain.'
Your gods are tennis-playing, sensual humans
Whom gold and silver heavenly light illumines.

What a vast difference in point of view!
In style! in everything!" Papend was touched by
This friendship, which, for him, was something new,
Since he had thought, as days and hours rushed by,
Only of getting power. Not many do,
But when somebody wants it, one is struck by
How little else he thinks about. Now, living
Here happily in Venice had been giving

This man the time to think and to consider
Just where his life was leading. It is sure a
Man in his middle years, once a great kidder,
May find himself *in una selva oscura*
And try to run off with the baby sitter
Or take up Taoism and tempura
Or of too many cocktails be concocter—
Until at last he's taken to a doctor.

Or, he may simply *think*, till things break clear,
As midst the Muscovites when summer breaks
By force of her persuasive atmosphere
The ice sheets, and the Russian heart awakes,
And, in the Russian wood, the Russian deer,
If there are deer in Russia. In any case,
Papend was one of these, whose intellectual
Powers can meet a change, and be effectual.

The Inca stays. But let us leave that city
To where Alouette sits on the Rathaus lawn
Of Stockholm, wondering why Zacowitti
Has not yet come to take and pass her on
As he had threatened to. She looked so pretty
I don't think I could stand her being gone,
So I am glad that Fate reversed its order.
She stares, then smiles at her red skirt's white border.

"Well, here I am, and, being here'll continue
To do what I was doing, search for Pemmistrek."
He, on the North Pole Train, was going in, you
Could almost tell, a new part of the haversack
Of what was in his mind. "If it had been you,"
He mumbled, in a doze, "Why, till the heavens wreck
I'd never leave you, ever." He gave a start.
His memory had come back! This was not smart

Or practical or anything while he
Was trapped in train on mountaintop above
The rocky world which snow gave unity
And he was there with Ann and others of
The Early Girls—he looked around to see
Just who he *was* with. He was filled with love
For Alouette, but all that happened after
Had gone completely, like a rotted rafter.

"Hum . . . who . . . and what—?" I leave him figuring out
What everything he finds around him means.
He looks into one door and gives a shout:
There are strange people reading magazines,
Whose speech and gestures fill his soul with doubt.
He strikes his forehead twice and wildly leans
Out of the window as the train speeds past
A polar bear, who strikes him with one vast

And snow-like, claw-filled paw, and sends him tumbling
Out of the train into the snow, where Ruffie
The bear, who'd thought he was a girl, stands grumbling,
While Pemmistrek leaps up, all fisticuffy—
But the huge bear runs off. Some ice is crumbling
So Pemmistrek, look out! He leaps above the
Crevasse. He's safe. And now he starts descending
As one whose story soon may have an ending.

Meanwhile a transformation comes about
Through a vague impulse animating Minnie
Who feels regret that she once had to shout
Foul words at Clarabelle. And she takes pity
On her. To Samos she had been shipped out
On a kayiki, months before. Now, quickly,
Minnie transforms her to a living girl
With some cow-like effects left, like a curl

That has escaped the coiffeur bent on styling.
She had been *slightly* human, always. Disney
Conceived her so. But now she's so beguiling
That friends expecting me tonight would miss me
If I knew where in real air she was smiling,
Her warm glance sailing to me like a frisbee.
I don't, however. Would I had a stipend
To resurrect her living from this typing

And be with her, wherever. Lashes large
As shot glasses, she starts to peer in languor
About the shore of Samos, where a barge
Waits, loaded down with works of Margaret Sanger,
Walt Disney, Kipling, Christopher Lafarge,
John Wheelwright, Proust, and Lionel Feuchtwanger—
It is the Library Boat! and on it she
Will pass the first days of her liberty

From almost total cow-likeness. This vessel
She went to, walked aboard—it was all outside—
And stood upon it, reading. Captain Cecil
Castikulokis, with his eyes and mouth wide
Open at the sight, felt moved to wrestle
With feelings that he was insane. Then, "Ouch! I'd
Forgotten I'd grown taller," Clara said—
For on a bargey beam she'd hit her head.

"Oh—Captain—you must be the Library Captain—
Forgive me! I am so unused to being
In my new state. Such crazy things that happen!
In any case, I ran here, upon seeing
These human books—I'm longing to look at them!
Oh could I stay a while and read?" Agreeing,
As it was easy to, to her request,
He smiled, bewildered. This was the first test

Of Clarabelle's (her less-cow name is Clara,
Which I shall call her henceforth) new-won powers,
Who, more than any cow in Connemara
Or deep Thessalian fields, where, gathering flowers,
Dis gathered Proserpine, herself a fairer
Flower than those she gathered, brought fresh showers
Of joyous perspiration to the forehead
By causing the whole person to grow torrid

Of any man who looked upon her face
And faery form, which now amidst the volumes
Of the library barge has found its place.
These human works will serve her as emollients
To help her flex her mind and fill with grace
Her slightest nods and gestures, which Italians
Some day will call, in thinking of her saga, ·
Gli atti amorosi della vacca vaga,

For all her gestures had a trace of love in them,
Something, well, indefinably Romantic;
And she stays on the barge, light currents shoving them,
Pursuing bookish pleasures unpedantic.
The Captain, as they pass, points out the Frothingham
Statue to her—she feels a tiny, frantic,
Warm pang of love! and they continue floating
To bring good books to each isle's rocky coating.

131

Landing on Chios, they behold a sight
Most unexpected: Mickey Mouse returned,
With Minnie, to the Race! Good God, good night!
Clara's embarrassed that her pale cheeks burned
In days long past for that round mouse. It quite
Undoes her. She but poorly has discerned,
However—she was terribly myopic
Since her strange change (an interesting topic—

Some physical changes still being uncompleted
From Cow to Girl). In any case, in fact,
The gala details that her vision greeted
Were part of a Propitiatory Act
To win the favor of the newly seated
Mouse members of Olympus. Wholly blacked
Huge papier-mâché figures, round of ears,
Being pulled past in a car, to thunderous cheers!

The car was even larger than the Packard
The mice had really used. It was enormous
And with red, yellow, white, and blue squares checkered.
Said Cecil, "It is larger than Pontormo's
Saint John Presented to the Virgin Backward,
The most extensive artwork, books inform us,
There ever was." Above it had been strung
Wires on which flowers and bits of cheese were hung.

And songs were ringing out from pink-faced students
From burly fisher-folk and fragile brides,
Lauding the Mouse's conscience and his prudence
And his tremendous driving skills, besides.
Assisting in these great Olympic ludens
Were thousands upon thousands. What divides
From all the rest a faith that's really living
Is just this sort of feeling, is this giving

Of everything, by everyone, to those
Who rule the Universe. And this one island,
The first of Greece to court the mystic rose
In Minnie's hair, led a return most violent
To the Olympians in loose-fitting clothes
Who, since Christ's Western conquests, had been silent
And close to sleep. Now feted, they awake
To passions new. Athena bakes a cake,

Apollo climbs a ladder, Zeus expands
His chest, picks up and hurls a bolt of thunder,
And Aphrodite, looking at her hands,
Decides she is a beauty beyond wonder.
It is the Mice, Olympus understands,
Who made it happen, and they are snowed under
With invitations, eulogies, and thanks,
And make a quick advance in godly ranks.

Mickey becomes the God of Everything,
A power superior to Zeus and Hera
As God is the superior of a king.
His Will determines all that in our era
Has any meaning. When you have a fling
With someone wonderful, or make an error,
Or drive into a cliff with your Mercedes,
It's Mickey who has done it to you, maties,

Or done it for you, as the case may be—
He is the Fief of Fate, the Lord of Luck,
The Duke of Death, and Earl of Amnesty.
His first act is reviving Donald Duck
In a small Cretan graveyard by the sea,
Who, once come back to life, hops on a truck
And speeds into Heraklion for a fitting
At Canard Tailors. Soon he will be sitting

Down for a dish of roasted man with orange
In a Heraklion tavern just for fowl.
Here, with his yellow-white face and beak of orange,
He'll think of Mickey, but without a scowl.
He loved the Mouse—no matter that the orange
Of jealous love had with an angry growl
Squirted him to oblivion! He was back,
Did not know how, but thought, "I have a knack!

134

There's nothing I can't do! I've lots of energy
And pluck and dynamism. What the hell!
I think I may go into plastic surgery
So I can help to make the shattered well,
Such as that Chinese fellow! It's encouraging
To be alive again and feel the smell
Of Cretan springtime soothing my proboscis
And see these duck girls beautiful as Toscas.

O life, you have been good to me! And, Death,
You too have been okay—since here I am!"
On saying which, he took a giant breath
And was transformed into a calligram—
Words everywhere feathers had been, except
His beak, which stayed the same, like Uncle Sam.
He was a "poetry duck" and not a real one—
Don't bring an orange to him—he can't peel one.

"*Pourquoi c'est arrivé à ce canard
De tant changer, en ce qu' Apollinaire
Appelait 'calligramme'?*" inquired Bernard
De la Hauteville, a Frenchman who was there
Writing an essay on "The Wingèd Star—
A True Greek Restaurant." Many would share
His curiosity, who saw that bird's
Whole breathy self being shifted into words.

The fact was, Mickey's power, being new,
Was also quite uncertain. Each commandment
Had some ambiguous words in it, like glue
Which stuck to what he said, relayed by cannon
To hilltop temples, then direct to you
And me by gnats and flies. What "like to man" meant
In resurrecting Donald—he had said
"Bring Donald like to man to life from dead"—

Was what remained unclear. Did Mickey mean
"As man would"? Man would do it in some art,
In picture, word, or music, and we've seen
The natural forces carrying out this part
Of what he said, confused, had tried to glean
The maximum effects: first made a smart,
Exacting, happy duck, far from acedia,
Then turned him to a high form of mixed media.

The words which make his feathers up declare,
I think, SOMA PSYKOS SEMA ESTIN,
"The body is the soul's prison." If you care
For intricate deep meanings, this has been
The best part of this story anywhere—
Think how man's language shuts man's meanings in
And is his prison, as his body is!
The French are very interested in this—

Too much, I think, but I confess that I
Am quite impressed by how it happened here.
So Donald moves no more, but now must lie
As art in the mind's inner atmosphere.
Mickey may see his plight, it's true, and try
To do it all again, but it's unclear
Whether he can or not. No need to dread
That Clara too will turn to something read—

She changed while living. Now in balmy weather
Of April, ten A.M., on Chios, Clara
Has slowly come to realize the tether
Of former love that bothered and embarra-
Ssed her need exist no more, for here together
Were not the Mice, but a Divine affair, a
Hail-to-Olympians scene. And now she trod
A stranger earth: "I-I once loved a god—"

She thought, and sighed. It seemed quite natural to her,
For in some books she'd read such things had happened.
It would surprise, though, most of those who knew her,
And it would mystify Commander Papend
That such a lady had felt flames all through her
For something seen most often in a trap end,
And now a god. His Venice had its own
Venetian gods, who loved canal and stone

And were not ever animals, but athletes
Who played Celestial Tennis all year long.
Nor would her story make much sense to Catholics
As they went mildly in to Evensong.
But it made sense to her, although a laugh keeps
Coming to her lips, which she thinks wrong:
How silly Mickey is! or was—who knows now?
And, Cecil bookishly beside, she goes now

In the parade, which is what it's become,
A long procession to the Cave of Egrets
On Chios' rocky top. Recovering from
Bad feelings, she looks forward with some eagerness
To the parade's excitement. Although some
May think that Clara shakes her cloudy ringlets
For Cecil's smile, in Cecil's bed at night,
They're wrong. It's all Platonic, which is right.

And so they walk along. And Pluto watches
Amazing star formations from his cot,
Where he's awake, although the "Buenas Noches"
And silence of his hosts show they are not.
"Good God!" he cries, as lights come down in swatches
To cover him and everything he's got
With white, delicious flames. Meanwhile the Butterfly
Five Hundred Sixty-Five has met another fly,

Not butter-, but a beauty, in treed Tuscany,
And they have set up household for the thousands
Of insect babies they will have. What else can be
So pleasant for such creatures? While the mouse hands
Of Mickey turn toward Minnie: "Millions trust in me
And have your and my statue up on mouse stands—
Yet still I feel . . . I'm guilty!" And, then, crying,
"What's power if it is so unsatisfying?

If only Donald could be here!" "He could,"
Cried Minnie. "You have, dear, but to command it!"
He did. Then on a tray of silvery wood
The Donald Calligram to him was handed.
What's this?" he wailed. He wept. It did no good.
Now turtles have on Mount Olympus landed
With numerous troops, and pistols, flags, and bells
And hostile mottoes painted on their shells.

DOWN WITH OLYMPUS! WHY SHOULD WE ENDURE
AN ALIEN RULE? LET TURTLES REIGN O'ER TURTLES!
AND GODS GO HOME! THE VERY AIR IS PURE
WE TURTLES BREATHE. WE DO NOT NEED THE MYRTLES,
THE OAK, THE BAY, THE SHINING SINECURE!
GIVE US OUR LIVES TO LIVE IN OUR HARD GIRDLES!
And other such. They march toward Mickey's mansion,
A Classical Greek Home without pretension,

Whose simple columns are the purest whiteness
That ever eye beheld and hold a cornice
On which a bas-relief extends its brightness,
To other art as fiveness is to fourness,
A very model of the loving lightness
The best of Greece produced. Secured from soreness
By armor hard, the creatures march ahead
Straight to where Mickey is. "What's this?" he said.

And they presented him their grievance. This
Was, fundamentally, that turtles were
Unfavored by Olympian emphasis,
And, being so, wished to dispassenger
From that transportative theopolis
And find their own. If this did not occur,
To live in an agnostic tortoise freedom.
Mickey with many well-picked words did greet them

Despite his sorrow. He was touched, himself,
By what he felt of kinship with these reptiles
Although he was, by birth, a rodent elf.
True, he had power now, ruled the skies and kept isles
From sinking down below the ocean shelf—
But, when he'd been but mouse? "GODDAMN!" He
    leapt. "I'll s-
Ee what the gods can do!" But at this second
A billion atoms to each other beckoned

And then a billion more. Infinity
Is hard to think of, but within a basin
Are atoms infinite, and those that be
On Mount Olympus wild at the disgracing
They suffered from a god's profanity
(Mickey's "God Damn"), suddenly started racing
Together, which explosions threw the Mouse
And his companion out from holy house

And home. Eternal Essence, though, remained
Unharmed, and other gods, who had been visiting
That day in Space. They fell near a two-laned
Hellenic highway, where Divine Necessity
Had thrown them, into a light blue mud-stained
Deserted Chevrolet, whose authenticity
Was shown when Mickey started it. He roared,
Unthinking, down the road, which led him toward

And into Sounion, where he is the Winner
(Crowds cheering) of the Race. He's made a record
In spite of everything, and Dr. Skinner
Of Canada Dry is there to greet him, tuckered
But happy, and invite him to the dinner,
Both him and Minnie, in whose mouse heads flickered
No memory of their fall or of Olympus,
Nor round them shone the trace of any nimbus.

They were two normal Mice again, as previously
They always had been, loving and intemperate
And full of laughter, sometimes acting deviously
And sometimes not, but hardly ever separate.
Mickey, afflate with Samian wine, inebriately
Starts leaning very close to Sally Everett,
A cub reporter for the Sounion *Nurse*,
And Minnie hits him with her beaded purse

And knocks him to the floor. But they took comfort
In being quite the heroes of each speech
Delivered through the night. They'd hear the one word,
"Courageous," then another, "great," in each
Such praise of what they'd done. How sound they
    slumbered,
You can imagine, later. With a screech
Trains run together. Pemmistrek's on one of them,
And Alouette's on the other. They make fun of them,

The station men who see them hold each other
And cry and laugh, and cry and laugh and cry,
Move back a little ways, then run together,
Look at the pavement and look at the sky,
And, as if they could really not tell whether
They were alive and really there, they'd try
To stand and stare but then find it impossible
To stay that far apart. It is unguessable

What thing in all of life could move them more!
Is this the True and Culminating Instant
At last? The sea is crashing on the shore,
And new events are moving in a distant
Part of the world we haven't seen before,
But these two feel, and are, perhaps, resistant
To everything, even the wish to know
What's happening now to others. As the snow

Of utmost northern Sweden, like the back
Of someone who's been standing at the window
Bare to the waist all winter long, and crack-
Less ice, like a long, endless prayer of Shinto,
Rush past the train unhushing on its track
One sits inside it seemingly akin to
A statue in a graveyard. Early Anne is
Bereft, alone. Then suddenly Atlantis

Reached up its watery arm to Ingle's height
And snatched the train with all the girls inside it
And all the others, to its hallways bright
With dazzling fish and sponges. The near-sighted
Conductor, Ingar Jensen, said, "We might
Be slightly later than it was decided
We were supposed to be. Something seems blocking
Our forward progress." Far beneath the docking

Of fishing boats, of rowboats, and canoes
The Girls are walking now, amazed and frightened
A little bit, it's true above the ooze
Of ocean bottom, on white stairways heightened
By rose and tulip shades, with some dark blues
And violet yellows which at first they mightn't
Have noticed since what happened was so crazy.
And Pemmistrek in Anne's young mind grew hazy—

She went on loving him but as a dreamer
Loves someone she has never seen in daytime
Sit down across from her and place the creamer
Within her reach, and sing some songs from *Maytime*.
So ended, like the future of the lemur
By further evolution, the great gay time
They'd had together. This quick transformation
By the Atlantic arm was the occasion.

Lonely Atlantides—the place had been
All men till now—had learned of their existence
('The Early Girls'), and, aided by a pin
Which magically did away with distance,
Had found the band of heavenly seraphin
Enroute to Northern points on pounding pistons
And forced an Ocean Arm to go and get them,
And loved them, as they'd hoped, the day they met them.

And so the Early Girls will love again . . .
This time I think it will be, in the silence
Of fabulous Atlantis, once the den
Of porpoise, then of people, city islands
Not simply cities they'll create when men
Care for them there, so far from any highlands.
And, sure enough, it is. Dear palm-tree places
Or little rock isles, which, like masks of faces,

Have one expression always, baby deserts,
And flat low meadowy places which are covered
Sometimes by water, and sometimes by pheasants—
With island urban architecture, buffered
By ocean breezes on their frequent visits.
So Hydras and Deer Islands, from the cupboard
Of Non-Existence, soon delight the eyeballs
Of seabirds fond of having nests on high walls.

Terence and Alma, meanwhile, like to those
Who seem to win but do not, still are straying
Across the roads of Greece, and, I suppose,
Will some day come in second. Monks are praying
Atop Mount Athos to the Mystic Rose
To speed them on, and orchestras are playing
At Schweppes's ballrooms that do not yet have
The news that Mickey has had the last laugh

And won the race, although he lost so much.
The Donald Calligramme, forgotten, glows
In a peculiar fashion, and the Dutch
Who hear of it from some newspaper's prose
Come capture it for their museum. Such,
To here, the fate of that bill, beak, or nose
Which once to Hu Ching Po meant such a lot.
Clara comes back to Samos, having not

Read all the books but quite enough, she thinks,
To make her happy for a while. The stars,
Meanwhile, lead Pluto to a silver links
Where he plays golf, and in the Theban bars
McShanes is buying everybody drinks
And rumbling happily. And now the wars
Of night and day resume, this battle won
By rosy dawn, which, festive, has begun

With various cloud formations, among several
One mirroring a white automobile
With pink reflected, in which Richard Feverel
Seems wrestling with a giant Christmas seal,
And in another huge one, light blue Chevrol-
Et-looking, seated at the steering wheel,
Elizabeth Gedall is learning how,
It seems, to drive through heaven. Later, now,

Clara, on Samos, walking (accidentally?),
Bumps hard against the Amos Frothingham statue—
Somehow this shakes him physically and mentally—
Entirely! back to life! He's staring at you,
Not merely standing there. Swifter than Bentley,
He moves, he holds her tightly now. Take that, you
Dull insect Death! And, hearing strange alarms,
He soars straight skyward, with her in his arms.

Noon hits the tops of trees and statues, as
The sun keeps rising, on its best behavior,
Over the White House, Rome, and Alcatraz,
And Second Venice where the light is wavier.
And in the garden they are playing jazz
And bluebirds bolt above the seaside graveyard
Where Donald Duck was, till his re-formation.
And to one reading in the railroad station

It seems, perhaps, that everything has ended
That matters to this story. But—it hasn't.
Strong impulses through the vague cloudbanks wended
And strange new energies became unfastened.
Huddel and Aqua haven't yet descended
To Venice, but prepare to, when a crescent-
Shaped car arrives, to take them to a feast
Where what they know of things will be increased.

They feel they ought to go. It is a plan
That may delay their voyage to the Andes.
It seems beyond the scope of living man
And is in fact the work of Nyog Papendes,
Who rides through heaven in a moving van
And is the Lord of Sad and Happy Endings;
He was afraid his son might not approve
This evidence of his illicit love

And so, before permitting her to travel,
Aqua, to see him, found this stratagem
To meet her at a feast and to unravel
From lacy collar to embroidered hem
The dress of his desire as to how level
With Papend she should be, and straight with him.
At least, such was his first idea. His second
Was to raise Papend, too, and so he beckoned

And had his bugle brought. "I'd best confront them
Here each with each," old Nyog Papendes said,
"Here where they're in the state of mind I want them
The most to be!" And then, attired in red,
He blew his magic bugle, like a huntsman,
Which Papend heard on earth and, as one dead
Escaping human hands outstretched to hold him,
Rose in the air. Canals below him told him

That he was going up and leaving mondo
Mas delicado for an unknown region,
A place where there were no gondoles to run to
Or walk about in furs to shoot a pigeon—
And now the Adriatic seems a pond, though
One knows how large it is upon occasion
When in a vaporetto to Torcello
Going as slowly as a spoon in jello.

And so, away he goes. He leaves behind him
The earth's most lovely women. One may question,
As he does, with this curious rise assigned him
By unknown fates, if his life was the best one
That man could lead on earth. Good-byes remind him
Of all the girls he leaves, and the suggestion
Is planted in his mind that they perhaps
Could have been happier with more numerous chaps,

One man to love each one. He thought, "I'll think of it
When I come back." He had the confidence
And lack of fear of death though on the brink of it
That power gives, like that of innocence—
He knew that he'd come back and I will drink to it
Because my liking for him is immense.
He starts to wonder, too, if his one use
Of women (love) might not be an abuse

Of complex natures for a single tone.
And yet the girls seemed happy. It may be
There was an aspect of Peruvian stone
Which, flaking almost imperceptibly
Changed human nature so that love alone
And such a love as his brought ecstasy
And nothing else came near it. High above
His duplicated city thinking of

These further aspects of his curious life
He wondered, too, about the vasty number
Of girls he wanted. Why not take a wife?
Someone to grow attached to in one's slumber
And be with always, shining like a knife
With faithful passion? Just then a cucumber
Sailed past and almost hit him. He was going
Now through a place where sky legumes were growing,

Not that where Aqua was but quite another—
There are, it's said, six hundred in the sky,
As much alike as sister is to brother,
Though sometimes different colors like a dye
Suffuse them utterly, so that a southern
Celestial garden, such as that one high
Above Morocco near where Zagora
Stamps forth its foot before the la-de-dah

Of the Sahara Desert, where the Blue Men
Ride purposefully back and forth with articles
They wish to barter with some other human,
Seems to be but a mass of purple particles
Though one can see, if gazing with acumen,
The different products growing there. Sabbaticals
Exist for study of such things—but now
He passes through a cloud shaped like a cow,

Then into fading, then more faded, blue,
Until all colors are completely gone
And everything a quite light light-white hue
Like petticoats stretched out upon a lawn
To dry on Easter morning, when the Shoe,
Which children think the Rabbit has put on,
Has left its tracks and also precious eggs
To which the children run on trembling legs

And cry, "Why are there petticoats out here?"
In fact, there aren't. It was the mere appearance
Of petticoats, was frost, which, in the clear-
Er later morning sky is gone, as Terence
Was gone from consciousness, as from the beer
The foam is gone, as from the throne room Clarence.
And Papend goes on sailing through this ether
Where clouds, air, everything he sees, is see-through.

He goes on thinking, which, on such occasions
i.e. when one is in convulsive flight
Away from what one knows and with sensations
That mix the energies of day and night
May bring about the birth of those creations
All kinds of artists treasure, and they're right—
For thought in one particular place has limits,
Like thought specifically men's or women's,

American or Russian, old Chinese
Or Maoist, or, say, eighteenth-century thought
Or rocking chair reflections, thoughts of bees,
Buranian thought. Creators know they ought
To find new thought that is like none of these
Yet where to find it? It cannot be bought.
It can, though, be inspired, which is what changes
Are helpful for, and being among strangers.

He was confused, inspired. And he envisioned
A Venice so much better than his old one
That planet earth would scarcely be sufficient
To be its space—a silver and a gold one,
This Venice, which would be at once commissioned
On his return from Space (doubtless a cold one)—
And he would boat in it with her as cargo
Who was his sister, Aqua, to San Marco.

Now he was sailing through the strangest places
A person could. His mind and heart were shaking
More than the hands of rooters at the races.
I cannot guarantee his state was waking,
But he was wakeful in its dreamy spaces.
He loved the new conceptions that kept raking
The leaves of what he thought and felt, and passed
Clouds like great sails, without a boat or mast.

And elsewhere Huddel holds in firm embracing
Aqua, while space birds flutter on both sides,
As through the higher stratosphere's enlacing
Of cloudy wisp on wisp that couple rides.
The word has come to her that she'll be facing
Her father and her brother, whereat glides
Tear after tear of joyful consternation
Down her delightful nose, which concentration

Can no way keep from wrinkling as she's sobbing.
I wonder if they ever will arrive?
It seems to be much farther than a robin
Has ever flown, or car could ever drive.
Nyog may have made an error, that of dropping
Some zeros from the mileage number. I've
No knowledge of transfinite life-death distance,
So I shall leave them, without more insistence,

Enroute to where they feel it is they're wanted,
With stars about them now to left and right
And full of secret notions. Someone bunted;
Another threw a curve. It grew more light.
And high above the mountain ranges, stunted
By distance, they all, soaring in their flight,
Are fading fast, or covered by the awning,
Which everyone can see, of early morning.

About the Author

KENNETH KOCH's most recent books of poetry
are *The Duplications* and *The Art of Love*.
He is also the author of
a book of plays, *A Change of Hearts,*
and two outstanding books on education:
*Wishes, Lies, and Dreams: Teaching Children
to Write Poetry* and *Rose, Where Did You Get
That Red? Teaching Great Poetry to Children.*
He lives in New York City and is a Professor of
English at Columbia University.